"Another swoonworthy read from Tanya Eavenson! I truly enjoyed this story about Amabelle and Patrick (so glad he got his own happily-ever-after!). The characters were well-developed and the storyline was satisfying and sweet. If you love animals, you'll be pleasantly surprised to find just about every kind of pet possible in this book."

— AMAZON REVIEWER

"Funny, endearing, romantic. The characters grabbed my heart and made me wish their story could just go on."

— KINDLE CUSTOMER

FINDING YOU

ALSO BY TANYA EAVENSON

"This was the first book I read written by Tanya Eavenson. What a wonderfully written and intense novella! The plot is well-crafted and the characters have layers to their personalities and backstories. Anyone who loves contemporary romance with a twist of suspense would enjoy this book. 'Protecting you is a job worth dying for; loving you is a gift worth living for, and I want both. To my very last breath.' Wow. This quote from the hero of the book, Brice, says all that needs to be said about his character."

— MJSH

"I'm so glad I got a chance to read this author's work. She has a wonderful way of writing the characters so that to this day they are still fresh in my mind. The story had some twists to it, which I appreciated, and was believable and relatable. Carl and Hope are such a lovely couple and the supporting cast of children (and a dog!) helped bring humor and life to their relationship. I highly recommend this story for anyone who loves a sweet, feel-good Christian romance."

— AMAZON REVIEWER

FINDING YOU

TANYA EAVENSON

Finding You

Published by All Roads Publishing

Copyright ©2023 by Tanya Eavenson

On file at the Library of Congress in Washington, DC.

Scripture quotations, whether quoted or paraphrased by the characters, are taken from the King James Version of the Bible.

Cover design by Erin Dameron Hill

Finding You / Tanya Eavenson —1st ed.

Ebook ISBN: 978-1-945981-13-5

Print ISBN: 978-1-945981-16-6

I will sing of the mercies of the LORD forever: with my mouth will I make known thy faithfulness to all generations. ~Psalm 89:1

ACKNOWLEDGMENTS

First of all, I'd like to thank the Lord for allowing me to write *Finding You*. Over the past two years, my health has gotten in the way of my writing, but the Lord had continued to place this desire on my heart, and now Dallas and Gabe's story is out in the world.

I also want to thank my dear friend and critique partner, April Gardner. She has been my constant cheerleader through thick and thin, the good and hard times, and knowing she's always there is a true blessing from the Lord. Without her, this book wouldn't have been published.

And I want to thank my readers for hanging in there with me over these last couple of years. This book is for you. A reminder that whatever we face, we can trust the Lord with our lives. He is faithful.

CHAPTER 1

*F*amiliarity hit Dallas Campbell hard as she lifted a blue shopping basket from the front door rack of the grocery store and strolled toward the cereal aisle. Tonight was her last night in Graham, Texas. The sour thought did nothing to dissuade her from plans of grilling burgers for her aunt, though Dallas was certain she'd not be able to eat a bite.

She strolled down the meat department at the back of the store and grabbed two pounds of hamburger meat, then headed for . . .

Her brain stuttered. What else did she need? She paused near the seafood. All she could think about was the sale of her house and the finality of it all. Or how, by now, Gabe Langston was the new owner.

Hamburger buns! She headed for the bread aisle, her thoughts returning straightaway to curiosity about the man who'd bought her home. He'd flown in from Tennessee, signed the papers while she was in Wyoming, and then flown back out. She'd never met him, but what did it matter who bought her childhood home, the one she started her own family in? She inhaled a heavy breath.

It's time to put down roots in Wyoming, she reminded herself. She'd been living there almost nine months and couldn't very well continue to make two house payments. Or deal with the memories she couldn't escape from here in Graham.

Dallas forced her focus onto the last few items on her list before heading to the register. After setting her things on the conveyor belt, she glanced around the familiar store one last time. Her gaze caught on a man next to her swiping his credit card.

Brown hair, salt-and-pepper at the ends, peeked out from beneath his cowboy hat. Short sideburns framed his strong jaw. She could see just under the brim of his hat to the crinkles at the edges of his eyes, more telling of his age than the built muscle beneath his green-and-blue shirt and faded blue jeans. A tattoo with several claws, partially covered by a rolled-up sleeve, marked the tanned skin of his forearm.

He noticed her then, and her cheeks warmed at being caught staring. He reached to tip his hat, and the markings on his arm spread to reveal a bear claw. His left arm showed another marking she couldn't describe before it vanished beneath his sleeve.

"Ma'am." His voice was deep, raspy even, and her heart did a funny dance within her chest.

She gave a slight smile in embarrassment, and his gaze lingered, falling to her mouth. She looked away, catching sight of a girl, maybe seven or eight, at the man's side, gripping the shopping cart's handle.

"Come on, Cin. Let's head home." The cowboy's smile

edged at the corners as he looked to Dallas a final time before his long strides guided him and the girl away.

Betsy, the cashier, swiped the hamburger buns over the scanner. "Dallas, how are you today?"

She cleared her throat and focused on Betsy as she bagged the buns. She hoped the embarrassment burning her face wasn't as visible as it felt. "Doing well, thank you. How's your day goin'?"

"Steady." She finished ringing up the groceries. "Your total is fifty-seven dollars and eighty-nine cents."

Dallas looked back toward the exit where the cowboy had gone, then gave her head a little shake and counted out the cash from her purse. She shouldn't be noticing another man. Her reaction to the stranger was ludicrous, unsettling even— it was the first time she'd really noticed a man since her husband's death. She'd been married once, and in her heart, she'd always be. Thankfully, she wouldn't see this particular cowboy again. Wyoming wasn't Texas, and that's where she was going.

"We're goin' to miss ya around here."

Smiling, she handed Betsy the cash. "Thank you." She would miss her favorite cashier.

Leaving Graham would be all-around hard, but it was the only way she'd be able to move on. The memories in this town held her captive, as did the countless times she'd cried herself to sleep from the pain of losing her husband and daughter.

No. There was no going back. The papers were signed.

After two years, it was time.

$\sim$

GABE LANGSTON WOULD BE the first to admit it had been a while since a pretty face caught his attention, but the woman at the grocery store took him by surprise. He'd been mentally going down his to-do list when he felt, rather than saw, someone watching him. And watch him she did. Those stunning eyes of hers, hazel-brown if he had to name them, gave him pause. Not to mention the way those eyes took him in from head to toe. Her rapt interest had brought a smile to his lips, though he'd tried to suppress it.

Yes, he was a newcomer to town, so that might have been the reason, but it had been a long time since he'd nabbed a woman's eye. He wasn't a young buck any longer, and, sadly, everything ached—a reminder of his rodeo days and of the two surgeries where the doc had stitched him back together.

Gabe carried several boxes into the kitchen and began unpacking the coffee mugs he'd collected during his travels with the rodeo. A lot had changed since then, and here he was making another change. There was much to do to get his accounting firm off the ground in Graham.

Some folks had warned him that moving during the middle of tax season wasn't a good idea. He'd never doubted the wisdom, but when a buddy had called about a house for sale at just the right price, he'd jumped at the possibility. Thankfully, he'd been able to meet with his clients in Tennessee and train another accountant to take over before he left. Opening another office would be a challenge, but it was time for a change.

Gabe leaned against the counter, needing coffee, but he had to find the coffeemaker first. He nabbed a root beer instead and listened to the silence in the house. With Cindi in bed, his thoughts set up camp on the woman with the hazel-brown eyes. He recalled her flushed cheeks. Vitality poured from her, a far cry from the last months before Melissa's fight with cancer ended and it took her away.

Inconsolable after his wife's loss, Gabe had decided to move, but guilt wasn't far. Leaving Tennessee felt like running with his tail between his legs. That might be the case, but this was his and Cindi's new start. He needed to act like a father again—to live, for Cindi's sake.

CHAPTER 2

*G*abe stood at the far corner of the living room and admired the work he and Cindi had done over the last three weeks. Every box was unpacked in their three-bedroom home, except for the boxes that needed to go up in the attic, but those didn't count. It was time to celebrate.

He strolled through the living room to the hallway, where Cindi's door stood open. She lay backwards on her bed, feet on the headboard. He knocked on the door frame, and she jumped.

"Daddy! You scared me!" She plucked earbuds out and breathed heavily. "I could have had a heart attack."

At her words, he stood unable to move. His eight-year-old was growing up much too fast.

He went into the bedroom and sank onto the threadbare quilt Melissa had made Cindi three Christmases ago. It had been her first and last attempt at quilting. He pushed the sadness away and forced a smile. "I thought we should celebrate the unpacking. Let's go into town and grab something to eat down at the square. We can do some explorin' while we're at it. Whatcha think?"

Her mouth opened, but before she could answer, a chime rang through the house. They both looked toward the door.

"Guess that's what the doorbell sounds like. Come on, Cin, let's see who's here." He strolled to the foyer, but Cindi hurried ahead and swung the door open to reveal an older woman with wavy white hair cropped above her ears. Her smile was as bright as her blue eyes, and she held a pie out in front of her. "Hello," Gabe said, coming alongside Cindi. "How can we help you?"

"Welcome to the neighborhood, Mr. Langston."

Hearing his name gave him pause. *How had she'd known?* She held up the pie a little further, as if he couldn't reach. "Oh, thank you, Ms.—" He collected the metal pan from her hands, noticing the pecans layering the top. "I'm sorry, but I don't know your name."

"I'm Ruth Albright, your neighbor. My niece was the previous owner of this home."

That explains it. "Please, won't you come in." He took a step back, and Cindi followed, allowing their new neighbor to enter. He closed the door with one hand and turned to his daughter, passing her the pie with his other.

She gave a sly smile.

"Cindi." He met her eyes with a knowing look. She'd probably sneak a piece before their guest even left. "After we eat. We have company."

"Yes, sir." Her expression fell, and she padded her way into the kitchen with the pie.

He shook his head, turning back to the woman. "That girl would eat sweets for every meal if I'd let her." The older woman's gaze traveled along the interior of the house from left to right, taking it all in as if she was the building inspector.

"You've done a fine job with the place. You removed the wall between the kitchen and the living room. My niece will be happy to hear. She'd been wanting to do that for years."

For some reason her approval gave him a sense of relief. "Sorry I didn't get a chance to meet her. It seemed our paths never connected. If it wasn't for our lawyer, I'm not sure we'd be standing here now. When you talk with her again, please tell her thank you for us." Cindi came to stand by him and looked up at the woman. "Isn't that right, Cinnamon?" he said.

His daughter smiled at the nickname. She'd told him shortly after Melissa passed that she wanted to change her name to Cinnamon because that was what Mommy had called her. She'd cried when he'd said maybe when she got older, but what else would you tell a six-year-old dealing with the loss of her mother? Shoot, he barely made it himself. If changing his name would have helped take the pain away, he'd have done it in a heartbeat. Two years later, their hearts were still mending, and thankfully, Cindi had settled for Cinnamon as a nickname.

"Want to see my room?" His daughter looked at Mrs. Albright with pleading eyes, hands twisting the hem of her shirt.

Gabe's breath snagged on his broken heart. They were going to make it. *Lord, please help us make it here. Help us find peace.*

Ruth took one of Cindi's hands and gave it a pat. She looked up at him as if asking permission. He gave a nod. "Of course, dear. I'd love to see your room."

Cindi led Ruth through the living room and down the hallway to her room. "Daddy let me pick which room I wanted. Well, I picked the biggest one, but he said no, so this was my second choice."

"I happen to like this room, as did Lacy." Once they entered, Ruth glanced around with a wistful expression. White distressed furniture took up two walls, a desk another, but it was framed poses of Cindi's horse, Sunflower, that filled much of the room's walls.

"Who's Lacy?" Gabe asked. "If I remember correctly, the owner's name was Dallas."

Ruth's gaze dropped to her hands. She nodded, returning her focus to his. "You're correct. Dallas's husband and child, Lacy, have been gone for a couple of years. The reason she couldn't stay."

He felt for Dallas and his and Cindi's own situation and tried to redirect the conversation. "She lives in Wyoming," he said, remembering it being mentioned the day he signed the papers.

"A horse trainer by day and dinner show entertainer by night."

"A horse trainer?" Gabe stole a glance at his daughter, her eyes wide with interest.

"A mighty fine one. She grew up working on the Easton Ranch. She was an Easton until she married."

"Papa and I love training horses too." Cindi looked up at him. "Isn't that the ranch where we have our horses?"

Well, Cindi hadn't done much training, more like odd jobs, but they'd always done them together until Melissa became ill. Now they were just surviving. "That it is. I wouldn't have left them with anyone else."

Ruth pointed to a coin framed on her nightstand. "You like to collect coins?"

"It was a Christmas present from Daddy last year. I got to

9

pick it out. It was fun. Daddy and Mommy have a collection they started together too."

Ruth smiled at Cindi. "It's a great hobby. The next time you go to the Easton Ranch, make sure you visit their welcome center; it's filled with artifacts from the late 1800s. I think you and your father would enjoy it. Well, I should take my leave. Miss Cinnamon, is it?"

"It's actually Cindi," Gabe said before his daughter could contradict him, "but I call her Cinnamon, or Cin for short."

"And that's because I love cinnamon on my toast, apples, bananas"—she counted on her fingers—"oatmeal, eggs, chicken nuggets—"

Gabe chuckled. "I think Mrs. Albright gets the idea."

"I can see why your father calls you by your nickname." The woman grinned. "I'll remember that the next time I bring dessert."

"Oh, Mrs. Albright. Cindi and I are fine. You don't need—"

"Nonsense." She waved her hand in the air. "Just being neighborly. Besides, it will give this old woman something to do. And please, call me Ruth." She gently cupped Cindi's cheek. "Thank you, Miss Cinnamon, for showing me your room. It's lovely." She turned and headed toward the foyer.

Gabe followed. "Thank you again for thinking of us. That was very kind of you." He hurried to open the door, then watched as the older woman waved, walked down the drive, and crossed the street. After making sure she made it home, he closed the door, thinking of the last few minutes. Ruth was the motherly type, and he didn't mind one bit. He recalled what she said about her niece, and his heart grew heavy as he made his way back to Cindi's room. She was already in bed, pulling her iPad next to her pillow and turning it on.

He leaned against the doorframe. It was hard enough losing his wife; he couldn't imagine what Dallas had been through, losing both husband and child.

Cindi saw him and smiled. "She's nice. She brought us sweets. Can we have some now?"

"Maybe after dinner. Speaking of, what do you think about tacos? I heard there's a taco joint on the square. We can check out the town, then come back and eat Ms. Ruth's dessert. Whatcha say?"

"Can we go now?" She jumped off the bed.

He chuckled. "Put on your shoes, and I'll grab my wallet and keys."

"Hey, Daddy, can we invite Ms. Ruth to eat with us sometime? She seemed a little lonely."

He hadn't noticed, but this was his tender-hearted girl. So much like Melissa. "I think that's a wonderful idea."

CHAPTER 3

*G*abe carried a box of Cindi's old toys to the garage and balanced the heavy box on one hand while opening the door with the other. "Cindi, can you close the door?"

Footsteps padded across the kitchen floor as he set the box down. Cindi stood on the tips of her toes and leaned out of the doorway, taking in the stacks of boxes. "There's a lot of stuff out here."

And he'd been at this for twenty minutes, maneuvering "must haves" into the attic. "There is. Are you sure you want to keep all your things? We can always donate them to—"

"No, sir. I still want them." She shut the door quickly, and it slammed against his next words. He'd accept the subject being closed, for now. They were still trying to adjust to the move and their new place. He didn't want to put pressure on her to donate her things and regret it later, but as he stared across the seventeen or more boxes lined up against the garage wall, he told himself he should have pressed her a little harder.

Climbing the attic ladder with two boxes, he was more than thankful the previous owners had floored the entire space, and that it was large, since he'd moved from a larger house.

Once at the top, he ducked to avoid self-inflicted head wounds from the nails sticking out of the roof. Since the two boxes he carried were Cindi's toys from when she was a toddler, he took them to the farthest part of the attic, where the ceiling extended and he could stand at his six-foot height. The day before, he'd seen a heart colored onto the wall there, marking an area where a child must have played. It would be easy to find Cindi's toys later if needed.

Setting the boxes down, he smiled at the heart, but as he looked more closely, he noticed something written within the shape. He ran his fingers across the letters, and the wall shifted slightly.

Acting on a hunch, he gently pushed at the wall. It shifted again under the pressure, revealing two boxes—one large, one small. His eyes widened as he stared at the unexpected find.

After reading *Treasure Island* as a boy, he'd dreamt of hidden treasure. Anticipation blossoming, he drew the smaller box to him, and grayish books peered up.

One by one, he reverently withdrew the books, reading the faded lettering announcing them to be old school primers. He'd seen one before while searching the internet for coins to add to his collection.

Fingering the reading primer, he lifted the cover and read the copyright date: 1887. He withdrew several more from the box before his eyes landed on what looked like a gold coin. He lifted it from the box, and a grin spread across his face. It was a gold $10 Eagle from 1882. He found another gold coin from 1895.

What a find to add to his collection! Just what he needed. What else was in these boxes? He dug back into the box and was flipping through a Bible dating back to the 1800s when a nagging feeling caught within the pit of his stomach.

Lost treasure. But was it really his?

He knew the answer before the thought fully settled in his mind. He pushed away his need to go through the box's remaining contents and carried the two treasures down the attic stairs and stored them in his room. He picked up his phone from his dresser and dialed Ms. Ruth.

"Hello, Gabe," she answered after the second ring.

"Hi, Ms. Ruth. I found two boxes in the attic. One had gold coins in it. I was hoping you might call your niece to let her know."

"That's considerate of you to let her know she left some valuable items behind. But I think it would be best if you gave her a call. Let me know when you're ready for her number."

Gabe hesitated. She wanted him to call? Knowing Ms. Ruth was waiting, he opened his nightstand and fumbled for a pen and paper. Finding them, he put her on speaker. "I'm ready, but do you think it's really a good idea? We've never even met."

"Absolutely. I wouldn't even know where to begin explaining what you found. Oh, and the reception is bad where she lives, so I'll give you her other number."

After getting the number and saying goodbye to Ruth, he hesitated before dialing Dallas. It took a few rings before a man answered the phone.

"Is this Dallas Campbell's residence?"

There was a long pause. "Can I help you?"

Gabe wasn't about to relay the finding of gold coins to a stranger. He glanced at the number Ruth had given him, and it was the same, but she never mentioned Dallas was seeing someone. Could she have lost her phone?

"Is this Dallas Campbell's number?"

"Who wants to know?" The man on the other end was clearly annoyed.

Gabe rubbed the back of his neck and inhaled a long breath. This wasn't going as planned. "My name is Gabe Langston, and her aunt gave me her number."

"Hold on." Muffled noises sounded against the phone before the man yelled, "Anyone seen Dallas!"

PULLING ON HER BOOTS, Dallas said a quick prayer for tonight's dinner shows. They'd booked four shows at two-hour intervals.

Her stomach felt a little off with tonight's changes, but it had always done that when she played her guitar for the first time in a new setting. Why would tonight be any different?

She glanced around her small one-bedroom log cabin, which was nothing like the home she'd once lived in and certainly didn't hold the warmth it once had. She may never experience true contentment again, or a sense of belonging to another, but she was busy keeping her mind and heart from feeling. She was quickly becoming an expert at losing herself here on this ranch in Wyoming.

Dallas pushed her thoughts away as she stood in front of the floor-length mirror and stared at her reflection. She fixed the red bandana around her neck while mentally running down the timing of the night.

Ride with Penelope to pick up the guests in the sleighs.

Share about the horses, then Penelope talks about the history of the area.

Follow Jon and Hank as we travel through the mountains to the dinner cabins.

Hurry off and open the doors for the guests.

Help serve the hot cocoa.

Pickin' and grinnin' with Penelope.

Serve meals with the men.

Sing and play guitar.

Solo.

Hurry to the other cabin for another show.

Dallas pulled her cell from her jeans and checked the time. Twenty-two minutes until they pulled out. She grabbed her guitar from beside the nightstand and locked the cabin behind her.

Penelope smiled at her as they met on the way to the barns. "How's it going? Ready for your singing duet?"

"It'll be fun," Dallas said, but her words sounded forced to her own ears.

"Then why do I get the impression your words don't match what's going on inside that head of yours?"

Dallas needed to be careful about wearing her heart on her sleeve. She was about to come up with an excuse, but thankfully someone called her name. Yelled was more like it.

"Anyone seen Dallas!"

She turned to Ethan who was walking her way, and she asked him, "What's going on?"

Ethan gripped his hat within his hands. "I was coming to find you. You have a phone call. Frank said something about your aunt."

Dallas handed her guitar to Penelope and took off running toward the main barn. Frank stood just inside, holding the landline phone against his chest.

"It's a man calling about your aunt." Frank handed her the phone.

"Hello. This is Dallas. What's happened with my aunt?" There was a moment of pause, and fear almost tumbled her over.

"Ma'am, your aunt is fine. I'm sorry for the confusion. I never mentioned there was anything wrong with her."

Dallas bit back tears, and her legs almost gave way. The man rattled on about something as she leaned against the wall and talked herself down from the irrational panic. Aunt Ruth had helped her father raise her after her mother died when she was only five. The fear of losing her was nothing new.

When Dallas's brain finally shed the panic, she caught the man saying his name was Gabe Langston. "Ms. Ruth is at the senior center now, playing bingo," he assured her.

She swiped at a tear along her cheek. "Then why are you calling? How did you get my number? How do you know my aunt?"

"I'm the man who purchased your house. She's my new neighbor."

She inhaled a long, deep breath and tried to calm the beating of her heart. When she remained silent, he continued, "I found a couple of boxes in the attic, and I thought you should know about them."

Was that all? He'd scared her to death for some trinkets he found in the attic. "Whatever is there is yours. Have it with my blessing."

"Are you aware of what's in the boxes?"

"No, but it's your house now. I have no claim to what might be left behind."

"Dallas." He said her name with such ease, as if he'd said it hundreds of times. "Ma'am, I've spoken to your aunt, and I honestly can't accept. What I've found is valuable."

This was news to her. She'd climbed the attic one final

time before she left and didn't remember seeing any boxes. Was this man scamming her and her aunt? She pressed the phone closer to her ear to make sure she heard him clearly. "What did you find?"

"I'm not certain what all is in the boxes since I've not gone through them completely. I felt it was yours to do, but what I did find is very valuable. If you can return to Texas—"

"Texas?" She startled. "I'm afraid not. No amount of money will tempt me."

"Are you sure about that?"

She felt a touch to her arm and turned to see Penelope holding up five fingers and mouthing *minutes*.

Dallas nodded. "I need to go, Mr. Langston."

"Is there nothing that can persuade you?"

She chuckled, picking an outlandish amount of money, the same amount needed to transport her horses to Wyoming. "Seven thousand dollars."

"What you find in the boxes could be worth more. The only thing I can tell you is I found two gold coins and old books. Make your arrangements. Let your aunt know when you'll be flying in. I look forward to meeting you." And with that, he hung up.

Dallas stood there, stunned, with the phone clinched in her hand. She immediately dialed her aunt.

"Hello," Aunt Ruth answered a moment later. A voice in the background called, "O, sixty-nine." She was at the senior center as Mr. Langston said.

"Auntie, this is Dallas."

"Hey, honey. Did Gabe call you?"

"B, twelve."

"Yes, ma'am. He mentioned he found something of value in the attic."

"He did."

"I, twenty-four."

"Have you seen the coins?"

"I have. The boxes were hidden away. He sent me a picture on my phone. There's more, but he won't go through the boxes."

"B, eight."

"Bingo!" her aunt shouted. "I gotta go, dear. They brought books as prizes this time, and I'm the second to win. I'll have almost the first pick."

"Wait! Can I trust him, Auntie? Mr. Langston."

"Gabe? Of course, dear, or I wouldn't have given him your number. Come home and see for yourself. Love you."

"Love you." She ended the call and turned to find Penelope, Penelope's boyfriend Dave, and his brother Ethan waiting for her.

She suddenly was emotionally exhausted, and the night hadn't even started.

PENELOPE REMAINED silent for too long as she drove the Percheron and Belgian horses through the mountains after the dinner-shows. Dallas could sense the questions radiating off her, but instead of speaking, Dallas stared out over the freshly powdered snow, lighted by the moonlight. The two lanterns hanging from the sleigh swayed as they headed back to the ranch, casting shadows over the snow.

"Why can't he just mail it—whatever it is?" Penelope finally asked.

She'd had the same idea, but Mr. Langston was determined it was better for her to travel to Texas. Could what he found truly be worth the cost of the trip and loss of pay? Her aunt said to trust him. She didn't, but she trusted her aunt.

"Says it has high monetary value, but he wouldn't really go into details about how much. That I needed to see it for myself."

"Do you believe him?"

Wasn't she just saying to herself that she didn't? Dallas shrugged. "My aunt seems to."

"I hate to see you go. When are you trying to leave?"

"Not sure yet. I haven't asked Jon, but I hope it won't be a problem. Do you think he'll fire me?"

She waved a dismissive hand. "Not you."

"I don't see how you can be so sure. It doesn't look good when he offers me a permanent position and I leave, again."

"I wouldn't worry too much about it. I overheard him talking on the phone about you the other day."

Dallas squeezed her friend's arm and glanced to Jon, who led the other sled just behind them. Jon was the type who dotted every *i* and crossed every *t*, and his employees walked the line he drew within the Wyoming Mountains. "What did he say?"

"Well, I shouldn't be telling you this." She smiled but became serious as she pointed a finger at her. "Promise me. Promise me you'll act surprised when you hear."

"Yes. Now, tell me."

"There's a rodeo each year in the summer that Jon helps head up. He wants you to carry the American flag for the opener. And I think I heard something about barrel racing."

"Are you kidding me!" She glanced to Jon again and lowered her voice. "This would be a dream come true. My husband and I . . ." Her smile faded with her words, her gaze finding the snow once again. "We used to do competitions. It's how we met."

Penelope squeezed her hand. "See, the Lord is working. There might be money waiting in Texas. Exactly what's needed to bring your horses back with you. You have a great job with awesome co-workers"—Penelope pointed at herself —"even if I do say so myself. And soon you'll be getting back into the rodeo. Oh, and let's not forget a guy who seems to be waiting to catch your attention." They were pulling up in front of the barn, and she pointed out Ethan standing in front of it.

"He's caught my attention all right. It's hard not to when a man makes himself clear. You know very well I'm not ready for a relationship." The horses took them straight toward Ethan and slowed. The lights from the barn cast a warm glow around him.

"True, but if you gave him a chance, he might surprise you." Penelope brought the sleigh to a halt, and Ethan was already strolling toward them. "Tell Jon about Texas as soon as possible and think about what I said while you're gone."

"Hi, Penelope. Dallas." Ethan's gaze lingered on her. "I hope I didn't come at a bad time?"

Penelope hopped down from the sleigh. "Not at all. We were just discussing Dallas heading back to Texas for a few days."

"When?" He held out his hand to Dallas to help her from the sleigh, his eyes still on her. She didn't want to be rude, so she accepted, then hurried to unhitch the horses from the sleigh.

"Dallas will explain. We're still on for a late dinner?"

"Of course. Dave's in the office. He'll meet us in a minute to get the horses settled."

When Dave arrived, they all spoke easily together, making things feel more like they had been before Ethan took an interest in her. But the moment Penelope and Dave left to brush down one of the horses, Ethan was at her side. "You're leaving so soon?"

She took one of the Belgians' reins from him. Her voice faltered at the look of confusion that ran across his face. Ethan was kind, handsome, younger by three years, and had never cared to date seriously until now. He'd made it plain he wanted more than what she could offer. She wasn't ready, not with him or anyone, but it hadn't stopped him from pursuing her.

She nodded. "It seems I have something of value I left behind, too valuable to have shipped."

"When will you be back?"

"I'll only be gone a few days. Or a couple of days more if Jon allows it."

Dallas caught Ethan's exhale, and the white puff of air seemed to stretch as they walked. Was that a breath of relief? A sign of frustration? It certainly was the latter for her. She didn't want to worry about hurting his feelings or about what her future looked like. After her husband and daughter died, she didn't want to think about her future or the dreams she once put stock in and planned to fulfill with her loved ones at her side. No. Now her focus rested on the here and now. And friendship. Maybe she should remind him.

But not now. She'd take Penelope's advice and think on things while she was in Texas. Time away might do her good, clear her head where he was concerned, but just thinking about heading back to Texas sent nausea racing to her throat. Would anything good come out of returning home? The way Mr. Langston spoke, she'd be leaving with a nice sum of money, but was it worth chipping away at what was left of her heart?

CHAPTER 4

$\mathcal{W}$aiting at the Dallas Fort Worth International Airport terminal with luggage in hand, Dallas scanned the area looking for Aunt Ruth. She'd been concerned about her driving alone, but her aunt had insisted she'd be fine. Dallas had even offered to rent a car, but she'd dismissed the idea.

"Dallas."

She turned to Aunt Ruth's bright smile and hurried the last steps before hugging her. It was wonderful to get her aunt's motherly hugs again.

"I wasn't sure when I'd see you again," her aunt whispered, releasing her.

"Believe me, I'm as surprised as you."

"Is this her, Ms. Ruth?"

Dallas glanced to the owner of the soft voice, a young girl who now stood next to her, her dark eyes wide in anticipation.

Aunt Ruth tucked a strand of brown hair beyond the girl's ear and placed a palm on her narrow shoulder. "Yes, dear. This is Dallas. My niece." Her aunt turned to her. "And Dallas, I'd like to you meet Cindi. Or Cinnamon, as we like to call her. Her father went into the *Wall Street News* shop to buy some gum."

We like to call her.

Father.

Something seemed familiar about the child, but she couldn't put her finger on it.

Her aunt pointed in the direction of the store, and Dallas's heart almost stopped at the sight of the man striding toward them, recognition hitting her full force.

The cowboy from the grocery store. And his daughter.

"Hello," he said, joining them with a pack of gum in his hand. "We meet again." The lift of his mouth was easy, sure. He handed the girl the gum.

Aunt Ruth touched her hand, her brow furrowed. "You've already met?"

It took Dallas several heartbeats to answer. "Um, not formally."

"Then let me do the honors. Dallas, this is Gabe, Cindi's father. Gabe, this is my niece, Dallas."

Gabe's smile widened. "Ma'am." He tipped his cowboy hat in greeting. "It's nice to finally be introduced." His smooth smile and raspy voice were so alluring they almost drove Dallas back onto the plane, but she stood her ground and forced what she hoped was a smile to her lips.

"It's nice to meet you both." Dallas gripped the luggage handle a little tighter and looked to the child. At Cindi's bright smile, the tension in Dallas's shoulders eased. "You ready to hit the road, Cindi?"

"Sure. Do you want some gum? I don't mind sharing. Daddy says I'm being like Jesus when I share with others."

She held out a piece, wrapped in red foil. "It's cinnamon. You can call me Cinnamon if you want."

Dallas nodded and accepted the gum, her smile genuine. "What a cool nickname. I'd like that."

"Thanks." Cindi took her aunt's arm, leaving Dallas and the heart-stopping cowboy to follow along.

"May I take your luggage?" The offer was kind, but she needed to do something with her hands, and fidgeting wasn't an option.

"Thank you, but I think I can manage." She kept her gaze ahead, sidestepping a group of travelers. She quickened her steps.

He caught up. "How was your flight?"

"Uneventful. Thankfully. I'm not much for flying, though I seem to be doing it often." Accusation tainted her tone, and she felt sorry the moment the words came out, so she added, "Thank you for bringing my aunt to the airport. I was concerned about her driving, but she assured me she'd be fine. Now I understand why."

"It was only right since I'm the reason you're in town." His gaze traveled to his daughter and her aunt as they neared the airport exit. "Let me get the truck, Ms. Ruth." He strolled ahead and reached them with three strides.

"Nonsense. I need the exercise. Doctor's orders." Aunt Ruth veered forward, causing the cowboy's steps to slow back to Dallas's side.

Was her aunt trying to put her and the cowboy together? Dallas hoped not. She already had one matchmaker in her life, and deterring Penelope was hard enough. She swallowed her uneasiness, tightened her grip once again on her luggage and held it firmly in place by her side until they rounded the parking garage and reached Gabe's navy truck.

"Here, let me get that for you." Gabe collected her luggage

and lifted the tonneau cover over the bed of the truck. She quickly assessed the seating arrangements as her aunt waited at the rear passenger side door. If her aunt was truly trying to play matchmaker, Dallas needed to put a stop to it as soon as possible.

The doors unlocked, and Dallas quickly climbed into the backseat.

"Dallas, dear." Her aunt placed a weathered hand on her arm. "Cinnamon and I were going to discuss an outing we were planning. If you sit up front, you and Gabe can discuss what he found."

She shrugged, glancing at Gabe as he opened the front passenger door. "I know how you become carsick from time to time. It will be best for you to sit in the front. Besides, there's tomorrow to talk about what was found in the attic. Don't you agree, Mr. Langston?"

"Gabe. Please, call me Gabe." He gave a knowing smile, and something like mischief danced in his eyes. "Yes, Ma'am. Plenty of time."

"See there." Dallas watched as Gabe almost cradled her aunt into the truck's front seat. Maybe it was her imagination, but she couldn't help noticing the tender way he made sure her aunt was comfortable before closing the door, almost like a son to his mother.

"Do you want to play a game?" Cindi's words pulled Dallas from her thoughts. She faced Cindi just as the girl buckled her seatbelt and turned a sweet smile at her.

"Ah, sure." Dallas snapped her own seatbelt in place. It had been a couple of years since she'd played games with her daughter. "Let me think," she said, but the train of memories pulled at her heart. "You know what? You pick."

"How about we look for different types of license plates, and the one with the most, wins."

"Now that's an idea. I've never played that one before."

"Oh, I've got another one we can all play! *I'm going to grandma's house.* Someone starts a list of things to take with us, and then the next person adds something. We go around listing the items in order as they're said, and the first person who forgets an item is out." Cindi leaned forward and grabbed onto her father's seat, looking between him and Auntie Ruth. "Would y'all like to play?"

"That sounds like fun, Cin." Her dad nodded in approval. "You go first."

Cindi bounced back to her seat. "I'm going to grandma's house, and I'm taking a sleeping bag." She looked to Dallas. "It's your turn."

Dallas smiled, not only for Cindi's enthusiasm, but for the reason she was back in Texas. When she returned to Wyoming, she was taking her prized possessions with her. "I'm going to grandma's house, and I'm taking a sleeping bag and my horses."

"You have horses?" Cindi's dark eyes lit like fireworks on a late summers' night.

Dallas gave a small laugh but didn't want the child to think she was being laughed at, so she touched her hand and gave her a reassuring smile. "I do. I have three. Do you like horses?"

"Oh, yes! Daddy and I have three as well." She looked up at her father's eyes in the rearview mirror. "They're at the Easton Ranch. It's beautiful there. I wish I could take my sleeping bag and sleep under the stars." A dramatic sigh passed her lips, and it took everything within Dallas not to laugh again. She caught Gabe's watchful eyes, the corners crinkling at their edges.

"You know the place, right?" the girl continued. "Easton Ranch? Ms. Ruth said you did."

"I sure do." Dallas grinned, enjoying her time with Cindi and how at ease she felt with her. "That's my family's land on my daddy's side. My horses are there too."

Her eyes widened. "How cool. You have a ranch."

"Well, not actually. But—" She'd always dreamed of owning one and running it with her cousin Blade.

"Have you seen the stars at night?"

Dallas looked down at her hands, where her wedding ring use to be. "They are beautiful when the skies are clear. And the sunrises . . ." Her voice trailed off. It had been Lacy's favorite place. How many times had they gone out as a family to look up at the stars? To see the sunrises and sunsets? Too many to count.

That's why it was so easy with Cindi, because of Lacy.

Gabe cleared his throat. "Cindi, why don't we finish our game. I know I'd like a turn, and Ms. Ruth hasn't been given one either. What do you say?"

"Sure. I can talk to Dallas later about the ranch and her horses. Ms. Ruth, what are you taking to grandma's?"

"Bingo. I'm going to grandma's house, and I'm taking a sleeping bag, Dallas's horses, and Bingo. I know she'd like to play."

Gabe chuckled, then said, "I'm taking a sleeping bag, Dallas's horses, Bingo, and dinner. We'd be hungry after all that Bingo."

Dallas forced a smile. It was so easy being here one minute, then the memories . . . She glanced out the window to control her emotions. She'd been good at hiding them for some time now, but being here, with them, it was too close to the life she once had. A life she'd never have again.

As the game continued, Dallas gave her answers at the right times and smiled when needed, but her heart was no longer in it. She was keenly aware of the battle that raged within her: loneliness, sleepless nights, dinners alone in her cabin.

They pulled up to her childhood home, the same home where she and her husband began a family. Her heart raced as they parked, and her breathing became shallow. How was she going to do this? Be here? No amount of money was worth it, she decided a little too late.

"Home," Cindi announced, unbuckling her seatbelt.

Home. Dallas paused at the words before hurrying from the truck, collecting her purse and the small carryon she'd tucked at her feet during the ride. "Thank you for seeing us back," she said to Gabe as he came around to help her aunt out. She pointed toward the bed of the truck. "I'll just get my things."

Lifting the tonneau cover, Dallas gave it a second to make sure it lifted fully before collecting her luggage.

"Let me do that for you." Gabe reached in, grabbed her suitcase, and set it on the driveaway. He didn't release it. "Cindi invited you and your aunt to stay for a while so she can show you her drawings and photos of her horse, but there's no pressure."

Cindi and her aunt joined them at the back of the truck, but it was Dallas who spoke first. "Cindi, thank you for playing a game with me and sharing your gum. It was wonderful meeting you. And thank you for the invitation to see your drawings and horse, but can I have a raincheck? I think I'd like to relax after my flight."

"Sure." She looked to Ms. Ruth. "Can you stay?"

"I can." Aunt Ruth gave her a gentle smile, one Dallas had seen many times since her family's accident. Her aunt was a fierce woman. When she set her mind to something, nothing could persuade her otherwise, except when she felt a person's need. That was another side to her aunt that always surprised Dallas, and she saw it now, in her relationship with Cindi. What was it Cindi needed that her aunt sensed?

"Let me walk you across the street," Gabe said, bringing her out of her thoughts.

She nodded, though they said not a word as he carried her luggage. All she wanted to do was hold herself together until she was alone.

Once they reached the front porch, he set her luggage by the door and met her gaze. "It was nice meeting you. Until tomorrow." He tipped his hat. "Nite, Dallas."

"Nite," she whispered, glancing at him as he left. She leaned against the house, fishing through her purse for the keys. Tears stung her eyes.

LATER THAT NIGHT, Gabe lay in bed thinking about Dallas.

From the moment he'd strolled out of the gift shop and realized it was the woman from the grocery store, his steps had lightened. He could tell she wasn't thrilled by the revelation he was the man who'd bought her house, but there was something about her, a drawing of some kind. Maybe it was the way Dallas was with his daughter—open and kind—and the way they talked, as if they'd known each other all their lives. It had seemed so natural he couldn't help watching her in the rear-view mirror. But the look in Dallas's eyes as he turned into the drive, there were tears, and they did something to him.

He ran his fingers through his hair, trying to understand this feeling. Was he being selfish asking this woman to return to the life—according to her aunt—that she struggled to leave behind? He was forcing her back to face a past with a daughter close in age to her own.

He shook his head and squeezed his eyes closed. "Lord, with Melissa gone, I feel lost and flailing even with your guidance. But now I've brought this woman here—over mere artifacts—who still hasn't healed from her own losses."

Maybe the worth of the coins would give her a little peace of mind for her financial future. Maybe the Lord could use this time in both their lives in a way they never expected.

CHAPTER 5

*D*allas had wished to sleep in, but it didn't happen. Her thoughts wouldn't let her. Being here again, surrounded by memories of her husband and child, brought an ache as big as Wyoming.

Her dreams weren't much better, especially when a certain cowboy entered them. She'd been trying to suppress the conflicting images for over an hour, but they finally drove her into the kitchen well before sunrise.

And yet, with breakfast almost finished, Gabe was still there, memories of him trawling through her mind. How his sight snagged on her coming from the store at the airport, the tilt of his mouth when he smiled in her direction, or his watchful eye in the rear-view mirror while she spoke with Cindi. He made her feel self-conscious. It was an odd feeling, and she wasn't sure why it bothered her in the first place.

"My, did you wake with the roosters?"

Dallas started as Aunt Ruth came up behind her and leaned over the stove, where their food waited. "Scrambled eggs, bacon, grits, and pancakes? Are you expecting company?" She raised her gaze to Dallas, who felt heat rise to her cheeks.

"Good morning. I hope you're hungry."

"You know I can always eat," she said, pulling two plates from the cabinet and setting them on the counter before fixing herself a plate. "If I'd known you planned to cook so much, I'd have asked my bridge group to join us. Maybe you should call Gabe and see if they'd like to come over for breakfast. I'd hate for this food to go to waste."

"Oh, the food won't go to waste. Now we won't need to cook every morning while I'm here." Even if she had to eat breakfast for lunch and dinner, Gabe wasn't coming over.

Her aunt raised a brow. "Don't be silly, dear. You could at least text him and see if they've already eaten. It's the neighborly thing to do."

"I don't have his number."

Her aunt waved her hand. "I'll get it. Gabe programed it in my phone." She set her plate on the breakfast nook and left for her room, her calf-length floral skirt swishing about her legs.

Dallas noticed for the first time how her aunt was dressed. Granted, she always dressed as if she was expecting company, but she wasn't wearing her house shoes. "Is today bridge?" she called out as she fixed her own plate.

"It is." Her aunt returned and settled at the table next to her, then slid her flip phone toward her, leaving her hand extended, palm up. "I'll be down at the senior center until two this afternoon."

Dallas took her aunt's waiting hand and said a prayer for their meal. She could sense Aunt Ruth's gaze, but she tried to ignore her staring and ate a few bites before placing a text to Gabe.

Good morning, this is Dallas. I made breakfast and we'll have extra. Can I bring you and Cindi a plate when I come over?

Dallas set the phone down and immediately saw him typing a response. It came through with a ding.

That would be great. Thanks.

"It seems they hadn't eaten. You are a wise one." Dallas thumbed his comment, catching her aunt's smile.

"Aren't I always?" She took another bite.

Why did Dallas get the impression her aunt was up to something?

Fifteen minutes later, after saying goodbye to her aunt, Dallas stood on Gabe's doorstep with two plates in hand. She had yet to knock. Aunt said he'd made changes to the place, but would it be enough for Dallas to keep her emotions in check?

Yes. She knew she could do this. One step at a time. One foot in front of—

The sound of the door unlocking from the other side caused her heart to race. She wasn't ready for this. The door swung open, revealing Cindi's wide smile and tangled hair tumbling over her shoulder, reminding Dallas of her own daughter when she climbed out of bed.

Lacy.

Her heart constricted, giving way to pain within her chest.

"Are you okay?" the girl asked, her smile falling into a frown. "Daddy, Dallas doesn't look so good."

Cindi's shout demanded Dallas say something. Anything to excuse the stricken look that was surely on her face, but before she could mouth a word, Gabe was at the door, concern etched on his features.

"Dallas." He looked to the plates she carried and reached for them. "Let me take this from you. Please, come in." He headed inside.

She hesitated a moment longer before stepping into the house where her dreams, and the life she once knew, seemed to crowd in around her.

She had to leave.

"Cindi." Gabe returned from the kitchen and touched his daughter's shoulder. "Why don't you go get out of those pjs and get dressed, then we'll eat, all right?"

She looked up at Dallas. "I can't wait to show you my room. Ms. Ruth said it was Lacy's. I hope you like it." Cindi turned toward the hallway, and Dallas swallowed.

"Your aunt, she shared a little about your husband and daughter."

"I see." She swallowed again, forcing back tears. *How am I going to be able to manage this?* She met his gaze then and saw the kindness in his eyes as he took her in, searching. Whatever he thought he'd find there, he was mistaken. She was hollow. A woman with skin, pretending to be alive.

"If you need to go, I understand. I can bring the boxes to you. We can go through them at your aunt's."

He would do that for her? "You don't mind?"

"Not at all. Give me about thirty minutes, and I'll see you over there."

Dallas nodded, and her eyes watered. She quickly turned away and headed toward the house.

CHAPTER 6

*G*abe watched Dallas flee from his house and across the street to her aunt's, Ruth's words rushing back to him. *She is a strong woman, with a loving heart, but her loss has stolen a part of her. I'm afraid she'll never find it again.*

He was selfish. He could admit it now as the front door stood ajar from Dallas's flight.

He wished Ruth hadn't spoken to him about Dallas over the last month or shared things at times he thought inappropriate. He understood Ruth's desire for Dallas's wellbeing and happiness. What family member wouldn't want the same for their loved ones? But knowing about Dallas's financial instability and her desire to send her horses to Wyoming, he'd dangled the money just out of her reach to force her to explore what he'd found. Now she was here, and he regretted it. She was suffering, and all because he was interested in a couple of coins. Valuable coins that she would profit from, but his motives were wrong.

He ran his fingers through his hair and looked back into

the house. He heard Cindi laugh, and a growing sense of heaviness settled in his chest. He recalled the pained expression Dallas had worn at the sight of his little girl, a sure reminder of her own lost child.

How could he make this time bearable for Dallas? If he needed to carry everything he'd found to her, he would, because if stepping back into his house caused her such pain, he'd shield her. It was the least he could do for almost hogtying her and dragging her back to Texas.

"Cindi," he called twenty minutes later, feeling the need to explain why Dallas had returned to her aunt's. He carried the two boxes to the foyer.

"Yes?" She came from her room, changed and running a brush through her hair.

"I'm heading across the street. If you need me, call, or come over."

"Will you be home for dinner?"

"Of course. I'll be back as soon as I can." He turned to go, but his daughter's lips pinched into a thin line, holding him in place. "What is it, Cin?" he asked softly, coaxing her to look at him.

"Do you think Dallas misses Lacy as much as I miss Mom?"

Oh, how he wanted to heal his daughter's heart. How they both still needed his wife. "I believe so." His heart tightened as he leaned over and kissed the top of her head. "Lock the door behind me."

Gabe left the house, and the lock clicked behind him. He tried to think of what to say before he knocked on the front door of Ruth's house, but he was at a loss for words. All he could think on was the tears in Dallas's eyes and how they did something to him. What exactly he wasn't sure, but how could a woman he'd only just met consume his thoughts through the night and well into the early morning hours?

~

DALLAS NEEDED to get a hold of herself. Gabe would be knocking at the door within minutes, and he couldn't see her like this. She dabbed a tissue at her puffy eyes and took a deep breath, hoping to settle her emotions.

Surely, she didn't look as pale as she felt. Perhaps she did, but it couldn't be helped. Dread had tingled through her from the first moment Gabe called her in Wyoming, but now that she was here, with the memories of her family, and being near Gabe's daughter, a deep longing held her in its grip.

The doorbell rang, and Dallas glanced at the foyer. She might as well tell him she couldn't do this and get it over with. She inhaled another deep breath and set her shoulders to steel her nerves. She could talk to him without being emotional. She was capable enough to speak to the man about why being here was a mistake. One that was too late to change.

She opened the door to find a solemn expression on Gabe's face as he moved into the house, holding two browned boxes. "I promised I'd bring them." He went into the dining room, set the boxes on the table, and turned to her. Gone was the smile that had seemed branded on his lips from the moment they'd met. Instead, his mouth pulled into a tight line, and his eyes held hers, almost pleading. "I've come to mend this between us."

What was between them? She wasn't sure, but she stood ready to hear him out. It was better than the turmoil sweeping through her. Afraid to speak, she gave him a nod to go on.

"I know now I was wrong for askin' you here."

Taken aback by his words, she was certain her facial expression showed her surprise.

He shoved his hands in his jean pockets. "I'm a selfish man, Dallas. My wife made it clear when I was with the rodeo, but that fact hit me hard when Melissa became ill. I lost so much time with her and Cindi, being on the road. It was a dream of mine, and I pursued it like a wild stallion. It's the same motivation that brought you back to Graham. I saw your coins and wanted them for myself. I had a feeling once you got here, you'd be happy to sell me the coins, with me finding them and all. And with what Ruth said . . ."

"And what did she say?"

He looked away, but she caught what seemed like guilt in his eyes. "She told me about your family, why you moved, and how you needed funds to carry your horses to Wyoming."

Her heart dropped, and a buzz of frustration hummed through her. Why did her aunt feel the need to share her personal life with a stranger? How had this become about her? "Are the coins that important to you? That you would bring me here to face my past?"

"Not anymore." His voice lowered. "I was wrong, Dallas." His whispered words felt like a caress, and her name on his lips brushed against her heart. "Will you forgive me?"

His gaze sought hers, and her frustration dissipated. Oh, how she wanted to respond in anger, yet there was none, only an openness that left her wanting. But before she could make sense of the odd feeling growing within her chest, he frowned. "I should go." He turned and headed for the foyer. "You can leave the boxes with Ruth when you're finished. For whatever you discover within those boxes of value, find a coin collector or auction house. You'll get your horses to Wyoming."

At his words, she realized she'd never answered him, but how could she? She didn't know this man, and hearing his confession left her mute and confused.

He reached the door, his hand still on the handle. He didn't turn to her. "Take care of yourself."

She watched him leave, her feet unmoving. Her mind and heart raced with conflicting emotions, chasing her like a bull, forcing her into action. She hurried through the doorway. He was walking up his driveway. "Gabe!" She yelled out his name on impulse. His steps slowed, and time seemed to stand still before he turned and began moving toward her.

Maybe it was better they parted ways. She'd tell him she forgave him, and he owed her nothing in return. Yes, being in each other's company would bring nothing but disaster.

Barefooted, Dallas took the front steps and moved toward him over the lawn, the grass against her toes bringing yet another memory. She inhaled a calming breath as Gabe reached her. "Lacy loved running around on this grass without shoes on. She said Aunt Ruth's yard was softer than ours."

"I'd like to hear more about Lacy and your husband."

She looked into his eyes, past the beauty of them, and really looked, and what she saw there was both compassion and understanding. Yet, she didn't understand the calmness settling inside her. She accepted it though and was even grateful for its return. "I forgive you."

His eyes widened. "Truly?"

"Yes." Maybe it wasn't better if they parted ways. Maybe with Gabe as a friend, she could get through this visit with her heart and soul still intact, no matter how tattered and fractured they were.

She glanced away from his penetrating gaze. "Would you like to come in? It seems we have some boxes to sift through."

"Yes, ma'am. I'd be delighted."

CHAPTER 7

*I*t was strange having a man that wasn't her husband sitting rather close, so close her knee and arm had bumped his several times as they rummaged through the first box from the attic. They found wooden toys, *McGuffey's Eclectic Primers*, and at the bottom of the box, several photos. She pulled them out, and the thin cardboard material of the photos reminded her of the ones at the Easton's Ranch. "Look at these." She leaned toward him, making sure not to knock against him again. "The ranch has some on display in the welcome center."

"Cindi and I saw pictures when we were there. This type of photo was popular back in the day. I can't remember what it was called."

"A postcard if I'm not mistaken. This one here is of Trent and Rosalind Easton and their three children standing in front of the tree at the entrance to the ranch."

"I don't remember seeing a tree."

"It stood in front of the property until a storm brought it down several years ago. Trent had engraved their names in the tree with a heart." She pointed at the photo. "If you look closely here, you can see the heart."

"Interesting. There was a framed drawing of the ranch from 1889 at the welcome center. It mentioned Trent had built the ranch for his wife."

"He built part of the ranch with Rosalind in mind for their future. The main house on the ranch is the original building. It's strange to think about my family's legacy starting out with a love story in Boston and settling in Texas."

"Are you a romantic?"

"Well, maybe. I used to be, anyway." She cleared her throat and shifted through the postcards. "There were some tragedies though. Rosalind's mother passed, and her father tried to pay off his gambling debts by giving her hand in marriage to a cunning older man. From what I understand, he was nothing but evil."

She stopped and held out a photo of the sunflower field Trent made for Rosalind. Gabe took it as she continued through the pictures. "I can't remember why Trent came back to Boston to see her, but when he found out the love of his life was being forced to marry another, Trent and Rosalind said their vows in the black of night and fled to Texas. To the Easton Ranch."

"At the Easton Ranch where my horses are stabled today. I'm intrigued by your family's history." Gabe handed her back the photo and leaned back in his chair. "What happened to the man her father basically sold her to? Did he end up in Texas?"

"He did."

"What happened?"

"I'm not going to tell you. Your answer is at the welcome center." She gave him a teasing smile.

"Tomorrow when Cindi and I head out to the ranch, I think we'll take a better look at the memorabilia. Did you know there was a photo of your house?"

She looked down at the rest of the photos in her hand, sliding one after another, quicker than before, not really looking at them. This wasn't a conversation she wanted to have. "The house was my dad's great-grandfather's. It was handed down over the years to one of the sons in their family, but since I'm the only child, it was given to me at Dad's passing. I grew up in that house. Married in that house. Brought Lacy into the world there. Through the curtains, I watched my husband and daughter leave for the last . . ."

Her words trailed off as her hands stilled. "At the memories of my family, of what we shared there, I can't help the tears. There are heart-wrenching days when I'm afraid to press on without them. Then there are days I wish time would pass more quickly so the pain would lessen." Emotion thickened her voice, and there was no use trying to hide it.

Gabe reached over and covered the hand she rested in her lap. "It's ok."

It was a simple phrase, two-letter words, and yet, it was more. Her heart took strength, and her mouth followed. "I'm a mess, Gabe. Broken. I can't pull myself back together. And if I could, I don't know how to begin."

"Then don't. Be a mess. Take one day at a time. But never forget the Lord is with you. It took some time for me to get my feet under me after Melissa's passing. Two years. She had pancreatic cancer, and it was a hard blow. Within six months, she was gone."

"I'm so sorry."

Gabe nodded, his brows drawing together, his eyes misty. "I have a lot of regrets. I fight tooth and nail not to look back on the times I wasn't there for her before her cancer. It changed me. She changed me. I'm a better man now, but it's a little too late."

Dallas looked down at their joint hands and his fingers wrapping around hers. She understood regret. She should have gone that night to take Lacy to her friend's house, but she was tired and asked her husband to go instead.

"We can't change the past, Dallas." She turned her head to see Gabe watching her. The pain in his eyes softened as he spoke. "All we can do is continue to move forward."

"I'm trying."

He gently squeezed her hand. "It's the reason I'd like to buy the two coins I mentioned. Melissa and I started a collection together. It's the last two coins we needed."

"Then they're yours," she said in earnest.

His gaze met hers, and she couldn't look away. Up close, his eyes were a rich blue that, given time to truly appreciate, she could get lost in. At the acknowledgment, she moved her hands from his. She had to direct their conversation from painful memories to a topic she could handle. "Speaking of coins, I'd like to at least set my eyes on them before handing them over."

Gabe seemed to have understood her need, for he rose and picked up the empty box. "Then let's get back to it." Gabe carried it away, setting it on the kitchen counter before placing the next box on the table. "I promise there are coins in here."

Dallas pulled out a worn Bible. "Are you sure?" She smiled as she examined the hard cover etched in a gold pattern around the edges. On instinct, she held it up to her nose and inhaled the musty scent.

"Do you normally smell your books?"

She smiled, embarrassed. She hadn't realized what she'd

been doing. "Why? Don't you smell your books?" She exaggerated another inhale, hiding her grin behind the cover.

"Not normally. I might start calling you Book Sniffer." He took the Bible from her and sniffed along the browned pages. "Yep. Just what I thought."

She eyed him, suppressing a smile. "What?"

"It smells old."

She laughed, quite aware of Gabe's own grin and the way he watched her, his surprise. "I do laugh, you know," she said.

He said nothing to that, but his smile morphed into a wide grin that lit his eyes as he set the Bible beside the other books.

She looked into the box and carefully lifted out a coin.

"Hold on." Gabe rose from his chair and pulled open a kitchen drawer. "Let me get a cloth to set them on." He returned and laid out a dishtowel on the table.

She placed not just three coins on the cloth, but, after looking back into the box, she laid a fourth down.

"I had no idea." Gabe exhaled, almost breathless. He pointed to one of the coins. "Dallas, this is a 1908 Indian Head Ten Dollar Gold Eagle. And this one to the right is an 1899 Coronet Head Gold Ten Dollar Eagle. Depending on their condition, and with my amateur appraisal, they could sell anywhere from three to four thousand dollars each. The other two, the ones I'm interested in, will run, give or take, three thousand for both." He glanced back at her, a childlike expression splashed across his face. "Now aren't you glad I called?"

"I am. We found treasure," she said, ready to tell him she was thankful in fact, but the garage door opened, and Aunt Ruth came into the kitchen.

"What do we have here?" Aunt Ruth's arms were full of boxes of tissue, paper towels, and hand soap.

Gabe hurried to Aunt Ruth and collected several items, saving them from falling. "Have a good day at bingo?"

"I thought it was bridge day." Dallas moved two book stacks from the counter and set them out of the way on the floor while Gabe helped Aunt Ruth with the rest of her items.

"Well, we played bridge, but some of the ladies wanted to stay afterward for a special game of bingo. Gabe, do you mind heading out to my car? I have a few other things."

"Of course. Is it unlocked?"

"Should be," Aunt Ruth said, placing the items in different piles. "I think I'm going to take these to the ladies in the nursing home. I also won several blankets. They'll be a great addition for the ladies since they're always cold."

Gabe came in with an armful of new blankets. "Where would you like 'em?"

"The couch will be just fine."

Gabe returned a moment later. "I'm going to head out. I know Cindi is probably waiting for me. It's tacos for lunch. Her favorite."

"You tell that sweet girl I said hello."

"Will do." They walked out of the kitchen together, but Gabe slowed them to a stop in the living room. "Dallas."

She looked to him. "Yes?" She waited, and when he said nothing, she struggled to fill the silence. "Thank you for helping me go through the boxes." She lowered her voice so her aunt wouldn't hear. "For being so supportive earlier. I'll take what you said to heart."

"It's more than being supportive."

She wanted to question his statement, but her heart fluttered at his words, and it unnerved her. Taking a quick breath to calm her heart, she moved to the door. She couldn't describe the emotions running through her. Maybe it was the excitement that her horses were going to join her in Wyoming, or the fact once they arrived, she'd still have a little nest egg, but when Gabe followed her into the foyer and stood so close, her pulse thumped at a rapid pace. "Thank you," she said quickly, looking away. She pushed the conversation in a different direction. "You don't know what this money will mean to me."

"I have an idea." His voice was soft, close to a whisper. "Will you come riding with Cindi and me tomorrow?"

Yes, I'd love to, came immediately, but she bit her lip to keep from speaking. Spending too much time together wasn't a wise decision. She came back to Texas for a purpose, and now that she knew all that needed to be done, she had work to do. "Thank you for the invitation. But I only have a few days left, and it seems I have a lot of work ahead of me. As you said, I'll need to find an auction house or a private collector, and I'm not even sure where to begin."

"I'll help you."

"You've done so much already. I don't want to impose since I've taken up much of your time."

With a shrug, Gabe's gaze drifted off toward his house. "The contractors are still working on putting up walls in my office. As a matter of fact, the last two go up today. There's not much for me to do but wait. So, how about we compromise? You join us at the Easton Ranch. We'll go riding for a time, have a picnic, then head back, and as soon as we return, I'll call a few contacts I know. What do you say? A couple of hours. No more."

She paused, her mind shifting from one excuse to another.

"I know Cindi would like to see you again."

The excuses dulled to a gentle need that grew within her. Yes, she needed to see Cindi again. His daughter wanted to share her room with Dallas, asked to open her heart to her, even for a short time, and she would gladly accept. Even if that meant returning to her family home. "What time should I be ready?"

GABE WAS RESTLESS. He spent the morning with Dallas, and once he returned home, he was tempted to walk back. He couldn't stop thinking of her. With Melissa, they'd been friends for two years before dating, and then after a few years, they married. How could Dallas have such a hold on him within days? It was unfathomable. He didn't believe in love at first sight, yet he had feelings for her, and witnessing her tears, it was like a hot iron to his heart, searing him. He wanted nothing more than to take her sadness away and keep the smile that had lingered on her lips for most of the afternoon in place. And when she laughed . . .

He opened his Bible, fingering the pages. "Lord, she's a strong woman with a broken heart. Show me how to be the friend she needs as she heals. Help my feelings not to get in the way and my mind from doing anything stupid. You know I tend to act first and think about the ramifications later." At least he wasn't as bad as in his rodeo days. He chuckled. "Yes, I know, you're at work, continually molding me into your likeness, but if you can mold me a little faster, I'd be mighty grateful."

Continuing where he'd left off the day before, he turned to Matthew chapter five and started at the first verse. It was time to meditate on the Word, not on his feelings. Earlier, when he'd touched Dallas's hand, he was a breath away from pulling her into his arms, and he knew how unwelcome that move would have been.

CHAPTER 8

The next morning, Dallas lingered in bed, fiddling with the two coins Gabe was interested in. He'd said the four coins they'd found seemed uncirculated and that, having been hidden from the elements, were in excellent condition. Today, he was going to bring her several coin holders to store them in for safe keeping.

She smiled at the way his eyes had taken on a glazed hue when he'd held the coins in his palm, and how his eyes had brightened when he'd looked at her. When she told him she planned to allow him to buy the two coins he wanted to finish his series collection, he went on to share that the coin collections had been started with his wife and now would finally be finished. Dallas thought she'd seen moisture in his gaze.

She felt the impact of his fingers wrapping around hers and how a little thud against her chest pitched harder. She remembered it now as she thought about the man. How they spoke of their past, his wife, and her husband. She'd connected with him in a way she hadn't with anyone since her husband's passing.

Within the quietness of her thoughts, something deep within her heart shifted. She sat up quickly in her bed.

I like being with Gabe.

Uncertainty and confusion filled her about how her feelings were possible, but possible or not, she couldn't deny them. "I like being with him." She said it out loud to no one but herself, testing the sound. It didn't frighten her.

Dallas smiled, but it faded quickly. She was going to the Easton Ranch with Gabe and Cindi today. When he'd invited her yesterday, it hadn't occurred to her what the morning would bring. She'd known she was attracted to him from their first meeting, but this, enjoying another man's company, how was she to act? Maybe she could talk with her aunt, and Ruth could help her navigate through her feelings and how to proceed. Was this the first step of coming out of mourning? Would she ever be over grieving her family? She didn't think it was likely, but perhaps grieving looked differently over time.

Dallas reached for her phone on the nightstand to check the time. She had an hour before they'd arrive.

After dressing, she found her aunt at the table with a cup of coffee in hand, reading the local paper. "Good morning, dear. Did you sleep well?" Ruth asked.

"As well as always." She opened the cabinet and took out a coffee mug. She began pouring the strong brew into her cup. How should she begin the conversation with her aunt? Should she just say that she enjoyed Gabe's company, and ask her thoughts? Would Keith mind?

She jolted as hot coffee ran over her cup onto her hand, spilling to the floor. "Oh no." She hurriedly set the coffeepot down and began cleaning up the mess.

"Are you all right, dear? You seem a little distracted this morning."

That was an understatement. With a deep breath, Dallas pushed the air from her lungs, and her words tumbled out. "I enjoy Gabe's company, and I don't know how I feel about it."

She continued cleaning the floor, unsure how she'd face her aunt after her confession. Aunt Ruth's gaze sat heavy on the back of Dallas's shoulder, but Dallas ignored it as she stood and went to work wiping down the counters. When all was set to rights, Dallas washed her hands. With her back turned, she finally said, "What would Keith think?"

"Dallas." Her aunt came to her and lifted her chin to meet her gaze. "You rarely say his name."

"It's hard, but I needed to ask."

"My Dallas, come sit in the living room with me."

They strolled to the couch and sat, her aunt's tender gaze telling her no matter what she said or asked, she'd always be loved and accepted. "Keith wouldn't be upset. He loved you as you loved him, with his entire being, heart, body, and soul. Nothing or no one can ever take that kind of love away, but I believe the Lord allows our hearts to grow to include others. We need others, Dallas. You've closed yourself up for so long, and I've been concerned. You have such a loving heart, and it's time to share it with others again. I believe Keith would be happy for you."

"Maybe, Aunt Ruth, but I'm not talking about loving someone again. I could never allow someone else to dwell in my heart. Besides, no one likes broken things. People like perfect things, things that are whole, a work of art if you will. I have too many missing pieces, and there's not enough superglue in the world that can put me back together."

"Perhaps you don't need to be pieced back together. Perhaps you need to be loved just the way you are. And who knows, the kindness and gentleness of a good man might love those pieces, filling the spaces between, connecting them into something you could never have imagined."

She chuckled. "Aunt, you're such a romantic, but don't get any ideas where Gabe and I are concerned. We're not even friends. We're acquaintances."

"Yes, well, friendship has to start somewhere."

The doorbell rang and Dallas stilled. Gabe and Cindi were here.

GABE TURNED down Easton Trail Road and listened as Cindi peppered Dallas with questions about the history of the ranch. Dallas answered every question with a sweet smile and a yearning gaze. He could spend hours watching Dallas's expressive hazel eyes, with their little brown flecks, that danced when she laughed and darkened with strong emotion. And right now, he witnessed the type of mother she'd been because that loving instinct was focused on his daughter. Even when Cindi cupped Dallas's hand, she didn't pull away but grinned, serenity filling her features.

His thoughts turned over about what that meant, and it brought a warmth to his heart. He'd imagined one day he might remarry, years from now. Maybe that would be sooner. He had to admit to himself, he hadn't known Dallas for very long, but he sensed this was the Lord's leading. Yet, she was leaving in two days. How was it even possible? How could he manage a long-distance relationship when he had an office to run in Graham and another in Tennessee, that he felt he was already neglecting?

Pressure from Dallas's hand against his palm brought him from his thoughts. He looked to her, then looked around when he caught sight of Cindi running into the welcome center.

When had they arrived? When had he parked?

He felt heat rise to the back of his neck and looked to where her hand still rested before her gaze drew him. "I was lost in thought."

"Everything all right?"

He nodded, enjoying the feel of her touch. He realized then this was part of who she was. When she sensed a problem or need, the desire to comfort drew her to touch. He shouldn't take it as being more, but his head and heart were having a hard time communicating.

He turned his hand over and cupped hers, giving a slight squeeze. "Yes, I was thinking about work. The new office to be exact."

She pulled her hand away, and his pulse ticked at a higher pace. "If you need to work—"

"No," he said, a little too loudly. He smiled in embarrassment. "Cindi has been asking me all week to come. I couldn't disappoint her." He'd done enough of that in her lifetime. "Come on, Wyoming. Let's get you back to your Texas roots." He caught her smile before descending from the truck.

After entering the welcome center, Dallas went straight toward the *McGuffey's Primer* behind the display in the half-moon exhibit. He followed, seeing Cindi had already reached Dallas.

"Daddy said you found a few books in the attic boxes. Do they look like that one?" She stepped closer to the glass and Dallas.

"It does. I'm wondering if it's around the same time period."

"It might be," Gabe said, setting a hand on Cindi's shoulder. He glanced around for the photo of their home. Seeing it, he pointed. "Check out the house." The changes over the years had been many, but he wished he knew what it had been like in the early 1900s when it was built. It amazed him the history behind the people from the Easton Ranch, Dallas's heritage.

Gabe continued around the display, looking at the family photos. Dallas was correct. They were on postcards. He smiled, turning to find a photo of a graveyard with an odd caption.

Here lies Grover Richards from Boston, killed by Trent Easton.

Gabe took a step closer to the glass and read the words again. It seemed Trent succeeded in the rescue of his wife. He couldn't imagine what it would have been like living in the Wild West. His gaze found Dallas and lingered on her as she stood talking with an employee, Cindi by her side.

Gabe had much to be grateful for, and seeing Dallas and his daughter today brought on a need to protect all that the Lord had and was about to give him. He only needed patience.

Getting Cindi's attention, he waved her over. "Stay with Dallas. I'll get our horses."

"Yes, sir. She's asking about the book."

"When she's done, meet me outside at the barn." Gabe strolled out of the welcome center and made his way to Midnight and Sunflower. He had called ahead to make sure their horses were already saddled and ready for them, leaving them more time with Dallas. Midnight caught sight of him and walked forward to greet him. "Hey, boy." He ran a palm over his muzzle. "Miss me? I missed you."

The groom handed him the reins. "We were able to get everything set up by the sunflowers. There's a hitching post at the back right side of the garden."

He glanced back to the welcome center to make sure

Dallas and Cindi weren't in hearing range. "Thank you, kindly. I certainly appreciate it."

The groom lowered his voice, "Here they come." He moved past him and continued to the ladies, pausing at Dallas. He pulled her into a hug. She returned the affection, a large grin brightening her beautiful features. "I didn't think we'd see you so soon."

"I wasn't planning to return so soon." She looked to Gabe, pointing at the man beside her. "This here is Blade, one of my many cousins."

"Only the smartest and best lookin' one."

Dallas chuckled. "Always so sure of yourself. One of these days, a filly is going to ride in here and, hopefully, stomp that prideful side of yours down where it needs to be."

"Never," he chuckled, giving her a wink. "I've got Kona all ready for you. I'll bring her out."

She looked at Gabe, a frown forming. "You called?"

He shrugged his shoulders before lifting Cindi into the saddle. "I hope you don't mind." He wasn't sure if he'd overstepped somehow or not, but maybe at the sight of their picnic, she'd forgive him.

Dallas said nothing.

Cindi hugged Sunflower around the neck. "I'm hungry. Can we have that picnic now?"

At least he was sure to make one person happy in a few minutes.

CHAPTER 9

*D*allas wasn't sure how she felt about Gabe calling ahead for her horse. She tried to tamp down her frustration as she rode alongside Cindi, but it was futile. It could have been anyone ready to steal her prized mare. Blade knew better. Then why had he done it? And Gabe . . . it wasn't his place.

She understood herself well enough to know why she was taken back, upset even. Calling ahead was something her husband had done before their rides, and now here was Gabe doing the same. It was uncomfortable. Did Gabe think there was more between them than friendship?

Cindi smiled up at her. "I wonder what Daddy packed for us. This will be our first picnic here. Do you like having picnics?"

She swallowed hard. Lacy had loved picnics. "Yes," was all she could press past her lips. And yesterday she thought taking this trip together seemed fun. Now all she wanted to do was turn around and head back to the barn.

Cindi continued on about how much she loved the ranch,

and though Dallas felt the same, her attention was focused on the man in front of her. She was baffled by her emotions toward him: frustration, hurt, and disappointment. She took a long, heavy breath, and as those feelings dulled, there were others that took their place. She didn't want to feel anything for Gabe, but somehow, she did. Not only did she enjoy his company, but she also felt lighter in spirit around him, and she genuinely smiled. It had been so long since she felt joy bubbling within her chest that it came out in a laugh. And his daughter . . .

She looked at Cindi, sitting tall in her saddle, trying to be so grown-up. There was a strong pull to care for and protect her, but Dallas had been holding those feelings back. She wasn't her mother, and she certainly couldn't allow her thoughts to lead in that direction. It made no sense. She was leaving within days and had a life in Wyoming.

Gabe stopped at a hitching post near the sunflower field and dismounted. When she and Cindi drew closer, Gabe approached and held out his hands for Cindi to help her down. "Whatcha think, Cin. Like it?"

Her answer lit her eyes, and she smiled sweetly at him. "I love it, Daddy. Thank you for bringing me here." He set her on her feet, and she hugged his waist.

Gabe ran a loving hand across her shoulders, then down her hair. "Anything for you."

Cindi looked up at him with such love in her gaze, the scene made Dallas turn away. She coughed to hide the emotion caught in her throat. When she turned back to them, Gabe was on one knee whispering something in Cindi's ear. She smiled and ran off into the sunflowers.

"Where is she going?"

Gabe walked to her and slowed to a stop a few feet away.

"She's huntin' down our picnic spot. I asked her to give us a few minutes to talk."

"Oh. What would you like to talk about?" She glanced away, the emotion of seeing father and daughter together pressing against her chest.

He neared. "I think I might have done something to upset you. It wasn't my intention."

Her head lifted, her gaze finding his. She crossed her arms against her chest. "You had no right to call for my horse."

"If I overstepped, I'm sorry." He paused, searching her face. "Dallas, you need to know something about me. Sometimes I take the bull by the horns without thinking of the consequences."

"And you don't get concerned about being run through?"

"Not really. Not until I met you."

Her hands slid to her sides, and she blinked several times, almost wishing he hadn't said what he had.

When she said nothing in return, his hand lifted and brushed a strand of hair from her face.

"Let's mosey over to Cindi and have our picnic. And since we've opened a time capsule from your family's past, let's do this proper, shall we?" His eyes pleaded for understanding as he took a few steps from her and held out his elbow.

For the third time this man had stolen her words and muddled her thoughts. How was she to think straight when her mind told her one thing and her heart was so confused as to how it was to feel? But looking into Gabe's eyes as he waited patiently with his arm extended, she did the only thing she knew to do—tuck her hand through his arm and allow him to lead her. "I've always loved the sunflowers," she finally said, relieved her voice worked. "Next to the horses, it's my second favorite place to visit."

"So I was told."

Of course. Her aunt was playing matchmaker again. She really needed to speak with her about this. "Is that why we're here? Because my aunt encouraged you? Told you I've never had a picnic at the sunflowers before?"

He gave her a gentle smile. "Actually, Cindi's favorite spot on the ranch is here. I thought she'd enjoy a picnic with the flowers. I spoke with Blade a few weeks ago and asked permission. You can ask him if you wish."

Heat climbed her cheeks, and she looked to where Cindi was taking the food from their picnic basket. "Sorry, I just . . . My aunt has already shared a fair amount about me with you, so I just assumed . . ."

"Blade mentioned it this morning. I called for Midnight and Sunflower to be ready when we arrived, and he asked if we were having any guests join us."

"So, you told Blade it was me and he suggested getting Kona ready for the ride."

"Yes, but I was the one who agreed."

She'd overreacted to the entire situation. Was she so afraid of his friendship she was making something out of nothing? And Cindi's horse was named Sunflower. Of course Gabe would set up a picnic for his daughter in her favorite place. "Thank you," she said as they neared Cindi. Gabe glanced at her, but before he could respond, Cindi was happily chatting away. And how the sound of her sweet voice filled Dallas's chest with longing.

GABE ALLOWED Dallas and Cindi to ride out in front as both their mares galloped across the open fields. He took in the sight before him, how they both laughed and how their smiles were in sync. His chest swelled with love at the scene.

Cindi was a great rider, and her braid bounced as she went, but his gaze continued to trail Dallas. She was a brilliant rider, the way her body seemed to glide with each movement. The wind whipped through her long hair and waved at him to continue following. How could he not when at this very moment he realized he was falling for her and hard. He had to make this work, for his and Cindi's sake.

Dallas was saying something to Cindi, causing them to slow and allowing Gabe to catch up.

"There's an old bunk house and stream coming up that I'd love to show you," Dallas said as she brought her horse to a standstill.

They dismounted and walked until they came upon a crumpled building nearly hidden by hardwood trees. "That's where the cowhands stayed back in the day, and right behind it flows a beautiful stream."

As they neared the stream, Gabe noticed how fast Cindi was walking toward the water. "Patience," he said, collecting Sunflower's reins. "Don't get too close to the edge. I don't want you falling in, all right?"

"I know." She hurried off and disappeared into the low-hanging tree limbs beside the stream, where they tied the horses.

Dallas grinned as she walked beside him. "I remember how she feels. My cousins and I loved this place. Every weekend we'd be out here, catching toads, swinging on tree limbs, and jumping off boulders."

He looked the stream over. "The water's deep?"

"No. I didn't say we were smart."

Gabe chuckled. "Yeah, the age when the word 'fear' hasn't entered your vocabulary. Those were the days." He spotted

Cindi on a small boulder, staring down into the water. "See something?"

"Fish. Come see."

They all squeezed onto the rock and watched the fish, and a moment later, Cindi climbed back down onto the bank.

"Where ya goin', Cin?"

"To walk down the stream a little."

"Remember—"

She let out a huff and waved her hand. "I know. I know. Not too close."

"At least she knows you well enough to finish your sentences."

"I just hope she listens. She doesn't swim very well." He turned to Dallas, settling himself on the rock, keeping an eye out for Cin, yet wanting to bring Dallas closer. "What are your plans tomorrow?"

"To pack. My aunt also asked if I'd help her rearrange the furniture in the living room. I caught her taking notes while watching a DIY show. Something about Nantucket and the clean feel."

"Would you like some help with the furniture?" He smiled over at her, and unable to contain himself, he shifted his weight closer. "Unless of course—"

"How does noon sound? Bring Cindi and we can have lunch, then work in the living room. Be forewarned though, I found accent pillows in the closet. I think it's going to be more than moving furniture."

"I'll keep that in mind." Gabe looked to Cindi, then at the water. He had to find a way to tell Dallas how he felt before she left. A day, that's all he had, and he was wasting time. He opened his mouth to tell her when his phone chimed. He slipped his cell from his pants pocket and checked the text.

I'd be happy to look at the coins. I'm definitely interested. I'm out of town this week but back on Monday. Give me a call then.

He smiled at her. "Remember the auctioneer I was telling you about—Daniel? It's good news." If Daniel was interested, then the coins were as good as sold. He handed Dallas the phone, and her hand brushed his. Warmth climbed his fingers, and he forced himself not to take her in his arms for a celebratory hug.

As she read, the smile on her lips drew him. "Thank you," she whispered. She caught him watching her, but he didn't turn away.

His eyes had a mind of its own, traveling over her face, taking her in. "You're welcome. I'm glad you came."

She blinked a few times, her gaze falling to her hands. "So am I. It's been hard, and yet—"

"Dallas, I—"

"Daddy, I've got to go to the bathroom."

Gabe jerked in surprise. Was he leaning toward Dallas? How long had Cindi been standing there? "Of course." He stood quickly and helped Dallas to her feet. A hint of a smile quirked the side of her mouth.

CHAPTER 10

*H*er memories, they hadn't rushed over her, stealing her breath like a tidal wave crashing all around her as they once had. Instead, there were swells of emotions, longings for her daughter's hand in hers, her husband's kiss as she went to bed, their voices in the sweet sounds of goodnight. But now there was another sweet voice that whispered in her ear as darkness fell, lifting her heart. Dallas knew now she wanted to be a mother again, to give the love she had bottled up inside since her daughter's death. How easy it would be to pour that love into Cindi.

Gabe.

Thoughts of him were harder to control, evidenced by how much he entered her thoughts. She wanted them to be friends, nothing more, but she failed miserably at stopping her thoughts there. When she was struggling with all she'd lost and those swells of emotions would nearly overtake her, Gabe was there, keeping her head above water. And other times, his kindness seemed to pour over her and through her. She felt as if she was on dry land, sprouting happiness by his side.

But what would happen once she left for Wyoming? Was this only a steppingstone for her healing, or could this be more?

Did she want more?

Dallas walked to her mirror and ran her hands down her jeans, then fingered several wayward strands of hair, placing them against her black top. She'd applied makeup that morning for the first time since she'd been back and was uneasy about the idea. She couldn't help but wonder what Gabe would think once he saw her. She'd take it off if she had time, but it was only a few minutes to twelve, and he and Cindi were due at any moment. She'd spent most of her morning making homemade lasagna. She hoped they liked it. It had been her family's favorite.

She left the guest room, and upon seeing her aunt's smirk as she entered the living room, said, "Don't say it. Not. A. Word." She went to where her aunt was working to take the knickknacks from the glass entertainment center.

"Me, dear? What would I have to comment on?"

Her aunt pretended to be innocent, but they both knew better. It was best to change the conversation entirely. After placing the *Home Interiors* figurines in the hallway, Dallas returned to the living room to collect the rest from the bottom shelf. "So, what are we doing today?"

"Oh, not too much." The doorbell rang, and her aunt went to answer the door. She pulled it open, and Cindi was the first to walk through, then Gabe. His gaze caught hers instantly, and a smile lit his face.

Taken by his rugged handsomeness, she responded with her own smile. "Hey, you two. Lunch is almost ready. Another twenty minutes and then we can eat."

"Smells wonderful."

"Thank you." She tried to ignore how his words pleased her. "Until then, maybe we can convince Aunt Ruth to share with us what we're really doing today."

Her aunt waved a dismissive hand as she led them into the living room. "It's easy. We'll move the entertainment center to this wall here; one couch will go on the opposite wall; the other on the wall facing the kitchen. The sliding glass door to the porch will be easily assessable. Plus, it gives the illusion of an open floor plan."

"Sounds easy, Ms. Ruth. Just as you said." Gabe raised his eyebrows at Dallas as he set his wallet, keys, and Stetson on an end table. She tried not to laugh as she walked back to where the knickknacks were waiting. Cindi came right alongside her, and within minutes, they were done. She found Gabe moving small pieces of furniture out of the way.

"Need some help?" She and Cindi placed the pillows, cushions, and throws in baskets in the hall next to the knick-knacks. Once everything was cleaned off, she and Gabe lifted pieces of furniture and set them where her aunt pointed.

Dallas stood back and looked over the room, amazed at how rearranging the furniture could make such a difference. "What would you have us do now?" she asked her aunt as Gabe neared.

"How about that lasagna you promised us?" He nodded toward the kitchen.

She grinned at him. "Hungry?"

"Yes, ma'am. This cowboy worked up an appetite."

Aunt Ruth pulled out three large shopping bags from the hallway closet. "You all go ahead. I'll be there shortly." Just as Dallas suspected. By the week's end, this room would have a Nantucket feel written all over it.

"Then let's eat." Dallas led them to the kitchen. Gabe

pulled out oven mitts from one of the drawers and took the lasagna from the oven.

She wasn't going to stand around gaping at how handsome he was or how familiar he was with the kitchen, so she took out the large bowl of salad she'd prepared ahead of time from the refrigerator. After fixing their plates, they sat at the round kitchen table and Cindi took their hands. It was only natural with the setting to hold Gabe's hand, but when she saw him waiting, she hesitated. Her thoughts flicked to a similar memory with her husband and child.

Guilt.

It was pressing against her middle as she slipped her hand within his. Every instinct told her that if she took her hand from his, the guilt would leave, but a trail of tingles at his touch sent distress signals to her heart, begging her to stay.

Cindi began, "Dear Jesus, thanks for Dallas, Ms. Ruth, our new home, horses, cinnamon, Daddy, and for this food. Amen."

"Amen," Dallas said, sliding her palm from his. She took her fork, giving her hand something to do so she wouldn't fidget, and began to eat.

"This is better than Daddy's," Cindi was saying as Dallas caught Gabe watching her with an expression she couldn't read. He turned a smile to his daughter. "Then I best take a bite."

What was he thinking just now? She wanted to ask. They'd been together every day since she stepped foot off the plane, but it felt as if they hadn't. She wanted to really talk with him, find out his likes and dislikes, what brought joy to his life, and countless other random things that flowed to her lips that she suppressed. Maybe after dessert they might find time . . . to what, she wasn't sure. After all, she was leaving tomorrow. The ticking of a clock sounded in her ears, mimicking the rhythm of her heart, fast and steady.

She wished she had more time here to figure things out. Her mind was a jumbled mess with the grieving and the memories of her family, and the thoughts of caring for the people sitting next to her. And these feelings for Gabe, what was she to do with them? Would they grow if she stayed? Fade away if she left?

"Excuse me," Gabe said, looking to his phone. "I need to take this." He rose from the chair and left out the front door. Whatever it was, it must have been important.

"I guess I was lost in thought. I didn't hear the phone ring." Dallas took another bite of lasagna.

"Oh, it was a text. Can I ask a question?"

"Sure, Cindi. You can ask me anything." Although she said it, her hand tightened on her fork. What could Cindi want to know?

"Why do you have to go back to Wyoming?"

Dallas set down her fork and cupped her hand over Cindi's where it lay on the table. "Because I have responsibilities there. People count on me, and I don't want to disappoint them.

"But don't you want to stay?"

Oh, how can I answer that! "It's the reason I sold the house and left to live in Wyoming; there's nothing to keep me here. My family is in heaven, and I'm lonely here without them. I needed a new start."

Cindi's gaze took on a look of desperation as she looked to Dallas, her eyes near to tears, but she set her jaw tight with purpose. Perhaps it was to force herself not to cry, but when she set her fork down on the table and launched into a speech, Dallas was taken by surprise. "I don't want you to go. You can always stay here with Aunt Ruth. Don't you like it here? We can go ridin' together all the time. We can find different spots on your family's ranch to have picnics on. We can make a game out of it too. We would have so much fun together. Daddy, you, and me."

"Oh, Cindi, I do like it here. And I've had so much fun meeting you and your dad. I really do wish I could stay longer with you, but I have to go back. You understand, don't you?" A tear rolled down Cindi's cheek, bringing moisture to Dallas's eyes. "Sweetheart, please don't cry." Dallas held out her arms for the little girl, and she came, tears and all, and hugged her neck as tight as she could. Her squeeze was light, and Dallas hugged the child in her arms. Her own tears rolled down her cheek. "Shhh. It's okay. I'll come back to visit."

Cindi pulled back slightly, still clinging to her neck. "You promise."

"I promise."

"What did I miss?" Gabe walked back into the kitchen, taking in the scene, surely not missing their tears. He frowned. "Everything all right here?"

"Just some girl talk." Dallas smiled at Cindi and wiped her fallen tears with her thumb.

"You promise?" she asked again, loud enough for her father to hear. When Dallas nodded, Cindi smiled back and gave her another hug.

"Well, since we're fine here, I have some news. I need Ms. Ruth to know." He pocketed his phone and headed for the living room, collecting his keys, wallet, and Stetson from an end table.

"Are you going somewhere?" Aunt asked as she fluffed pillows.

"Would you both mind if Cindi stays here for a while? A main water line in the building downtown must have burst.

The project manager says that when they came back from lunch, there was water everywhere. I need to head there to figure out the damage and what needs to be done."

"Of course, Gabe. You go on. Cindi will be fine here."

"Thank you." He looked to his daughter. "You behave. I love you." He kissed her forehead.

"I will. Me and Dallas can play some games."

"I think I met my match. There aren't many people who love games as much as me." She gave Cindi a reassuring smile.

"Dallas, will you walk with me?" he asked as he settled his hat on his head, hiding his gaze from her. He held open the front door for her, and they silently walked down the driveway.

Once they reached the truck, she broke the quiet, unable to stand it any longer. "Is there anything I can do to help? I'd be happy to drive my aunt's car and meet you there."

"Thank you for the offer, but I'm not sure how long I'll be there or what needs to be done. The office was to open in two weeks and now that looks unlikely. I might miss most of the tax season." He rubbed the back of his neck. "Thankfully, I didn't close the office in Tennessee."

Dallas had a mixture of emotions. She wanted to help Gabe with the clean-up, or even just be near him for moral support, do anything she could to relieve his stress, but he hadn't asked. Instead, he'd turned her down when she offered.

Were these their last moments together?

She wanted to ask if he cared for her, and if he would think of her once she was gone, but the worry on his face pushed her to keep her thoughts to herself. She took a few steps back toward the house to give herself some space before she reached out to comfort him or said something foolish. There was one way she could help Gabe. "I'll make sure Cindi wins at least two of the games we play. Now you better go. I know you'll feel better once you get there and get busy."

"What time do you need to be at the airport in the morning?"

"I need to leave here at four. My plane leaves at six-thirty, but I'll have a taxi carry me."

"But I'd like to take you."

"How about we discuss it when you get back? Until then, you better get going, or you'll miss dinner with us all together."

He tipped the brim of his hat and smiled. "Yes, ma'am. I'll see ya tonight." She stood in her old driveway and watched Gabe pull away and head down the street.

How had her empty life become filled and complicated so quickly she didn't know. But tonight, she was going to complicate it even more by telling Gabe how she felt.

CHAPTER 11

*A*s Dallas and Cindi played board game after board game, they watched Aunt Ruth dust every space in the entertainment center and share facts about each figurine. It had grown dark outside, and there was still no sign or word from Gabe.

Cindi's eyes had grown heavy while Dallas was putting the *Candy Land* pieces away. It was time to take her home. "Aunt, I'm going to take Cindi to the house. Do you know what the keypad passwords are?"

"They weren't changed. Since you're looking after Cindi, I'm going to shower and head to bed. I think I've done all I can do tonight. I'll wake up and say goodbye before you go."

Dallas stood and kissed her aunt's cheek. "I'll be back as soon as I can."

Aunt hugged her, whispering, "Are you sure you won't let Gabe take you to the airport?"

"Perhaps if he'd returned, we could've talked about it, but I'm not going to have him feel obligated when I know he'll be beat after tonight."

"He can't be much longer."

She took her aunt's hands and gave them a kiss. "Thank you for caring for and loving me, but I think this is best. Besides, I called for a taxi, and thanks to Cindi's help, my bags are packed and ready to go."

Aunt Ruth squeezed her hands in understanding. She turned to Cindi, who was leaning against the couch cushions. "Nite, dear. I'm heading to bed."

Cindi yawned. "Goodnight."

"You ready to head to your house?" Dallas asked, collecting her keys from the end table where Gabe's were earlier.

Nodding, Cindi stood and took her hand. They crossed the street, and as they entered the house, Cindi asked, "Do you want to see my room now?"

"I'd love to." With Cindi still holding her hand and pulling her along, Dallas hadn't a chance to look around. She managed to lock the door behind her, then focused on her steps, though she did notice a wall between the kitchen and living room was missing.

"This is mine and Lacy's room." Cindi pointed down the hallway as they reached it.

Dalla's breath caught in her throat. Could she do this?

They crossed the threshold, and Cindi finally released her hand. She turned on the light and rushed to one of the many horse photos hanging on the wall. Ribbons adorned almost every frame. "This is mine and Sunflower's first blue ribbon."

Dallas nodded, taking a much-needed breath to calm her nerves. The changes in the room were many. Even the placement of the furniture was different. She forced herself to look at the photo and the eager child. Cindi's warm smile was contagious and eased her nerves. "You are so adorable. How old were you?"

"That was a little over two years ago. Mom was around then," she said casually as she went to the next photo, yet Dallas caught the sadness in her eyes. "I made this wreath of sunflowers with Mom right before she passed. I know it made her feel better. She told me. Though she couldn't go to the barn with Dad and me to give it to Sunflower, you can tell here my horse liked it too."

"I can see why you love sunflowers as much as I do. Lacy used to bring me sunflowers too."

"We're pretty special to have people who love us enough to bring us our favorite flowers."

"I think you're so smart for your age. Besides"—Dallas went to another photo on the wall—"I could tell you were a good rider. I just didn't realize how good. Your ribbons are impressive for a girl your age." She moved down the wall to the others. "You must have had a coach in Tennessee."

"Yes, but we don't have one here."

"I'm sure you will before you know it. Not to worry. I can give your dad a few names you might want to use." Cindi yawed again, and Dallas looked at the nightstand for a clock. After finding it, she took in the full view of the room and pointed to the dresser. "Why don't you grab your pjs and take a shower. I'll keep looking at your pictures, and when you get done, I'll read you a story. How does that sound?"

"I'd like that." She strolled to the dresser and pulled out her pjs. "Have you heard from Daddy?"

"No, but I'm afraid the damage is probably more than he first thought."

"I hope not, but you might be right. I know he wanted to spend the day with you since you're leaving, and it's after eleven o'clock." Cindi headed toward the hallway bathroom.

Dallas set her keys on the dresser and checked her phone. Seeing there were no messages, she texted Gabe to let him know they were at home, his home, and she'd stay until he returned.

Thank you, Dallas. This wasn't how this night was supposed to go.

You do what you need to. Cindi and I are fine.

Thank you . . . I'll try to be home as soon as I can.

She gave his last text a thumbs-up, because what else could she say? Each text from him pulled at her in different ways: first hope, that he had wanted to spend time with her; and then the feeling of home. That she belonged. Family. How that word once brought so much joy to her life. Now, the word "home" seemed at odds with her heart at just the sound, and when she thought of home, there were others that came to mind.

Dallas had to tell Gabe how she felt one way or another. She said she was going to do it, and while Cindi was taking a shower, it was the perfect time. Going to Cindi's desk, she rummaged around and found several pieces of loose wide-ruled paper and an array of colored pens. Sitting in Cindi's desk chair, she found a pen and allowed the words to pour out on the paper.

Once she finished, she read over her words. Though it was short, it was all she could say until she knew how Gabe felt. She folded the letter. Cindi came into the bedroom and dropped her dirty clothes into a hamper in the closet.

Dallas held out the letter to her. "I wrote a letter for your dad. Will you put it where he'll see it?"

"Sure. He keeps a place on his dresser for me to set things I want him to see or to sign for school. We're on spring break, so he'll see it right off."

"Thank you."

Cindi left, and a moment later, came back. "Can you read me to sleep?"

"What book did you want to read?"

She pulled a book from the shelf and crawled into bed, then held the book out to Dallas. "*The Horse of My Heart.* Daddy bought it for me, but I haven't read it yet."

"Sounds like a good choice, especially with us being horse lovers and all." Cindi snuggled close, and Dallas wrapped an arm around her shoulders.

"Dallas, I'll miss you when you're gone."

She bit her lip at Cindi's words, fighting the tears that sprang to her eyes. "I'll miss you too, sweetheart. More than you know." She kissed the top of Cindi's head and began reading.

GABE WAS A MESS. He was sore, damp in places and dry in others. Dirt and grime stained his clothes where he'd helped cut off the main water supply to the building. The new drywall had been ruined and now needed to be rehung. They had fans blowing in every area where water touched, and hours later, it still wasn't all dry. They needed to hire someone to extract the water, and there was only one man available in town, but he couldn't come out until tomorrow. Everything was ruined, even the time he'd planned to spend with Dallas.

Finally home, he quickly turned off the alarm and closed the door behind him. He went into the kitchen first for a water bottle and noticed the time. It was after one in the morning. He had to find Dallas to wake her and send her to her aunt's. She had to be at the airport in a few hours, and he suspected she had called a taxi to drive her there.

After washing his hands and collecting a water bottle from the fridge, he walked quietly through the house, drinking as he did. He turned on the hall light, then stepped into Cindi's room and stopped dead in his tracks. Dallas was sitting up against the headboard, eyes closed, head slightly turned to the side. Cindi was also sound asleep, with her head in Dallas's lap. His heart clenched tight at the sight of them together. He realized then he had failed himself and his daughter. Dallas was leaving, and he was letting her walk away.

Gabe went to the side of the bed, taken by how beautiful Dallas was while she slept. He moved her hair away from her eyes and tucked the soft strands behind her ear. "Dallas," he whispered, brushing a tender finger across her cheek. She stirred and he called her name once again. Her eyes slowly opened, and a smile played at the corners of her mouth. His gaze was drawn to her lips, and heaven help him, he was tempted to kiss her.

She began to move, then quickly stilled, as if noticing that Cindi was sleeping in her lap. She cupped his daughter's head as she slid from beneath her. Gabe pulled the bed covers to his daughter's chin, and once she was settled, placed a light hand to Dallas's back, leading her out.

"How did tonight go?" She stifled a yawn and blinked a few times. "You look like you got into your work."

"It's a mess. I'm a mess." He tugged on his shirt and inhaled a long breath. "It's going to be another month before we can open the doors."

"I'm sorry this happened."

"There's a lot of things I'm sorry for and one of them was

not spending the day with you. Or taking you to the airport. Did you end up calling a taxi?"

"I did. Besides, it would be easier." She looked around. "Oh, Gabe, I left my phone and keys on the dresser in Cindi's room."

"I'll get them, and then I should take you back." He quietly entered the room and nabbed the keys and phone before meeting Dallas in the foyer. "Here you go."

"Thank you." She looked back toward the living room. "I didn't see much of the house, but what I did, you've done a nice job with the place."

"Were you all right being here? I was a little concerned once I read your text."

She shrugged. "I had a couple of moments, but Cindi needed to be home. She was tired, and there's no better place than your own bed."

"Speaking of, you should probably get a few hours of sleep," he said, though he was anything but ready to let her go. These were their last moments together, and he didn't want to say anything to scare her off. They left through the front door, taking the walkway to the street.

"You don't have to walk me to the door."

"How could I not?" *How could he let her go?* "We're going to miss you."

"Cindi said the same. You have a wonderful daughter, Gabe."

They reached her aunt's door, and it took all his willpower to hold himself from taking her into his arms. *What would it be like to kiss her?* "Earlier tonight"—he took a step near her—"you promised Cindi something. I overheard when I came into the house. What did you promise her?"

"That I'd be back."

She was coming back to them. She'd said so herself. He took another step, his fingers itching to brush against her cheek, to twine their way through her hair. "You promised her?"

"Yes, my aunt lives across the street. Of course, I'll be back."

"Of course." His body stiffened, and he stuffed his hands into his pockets. What had he expected? He glanced back to his house to get control of the hurt and disappointment building in his chest. His emotions were on a roller coaster with the day he'd had, and he needed to end this night before he did or said something he'd regret. "I should go." At his words, her eyes looked troubled, but why?

Dallas bit her lip and nodded. "Bye, Gabe." She turned and began to unlock the door.

This was it, and he couldn't stay and watch her walk away. It was hard enough to know his feelings were one-sided. He loved her, and he wasn't giving up, but for now, he needed a good night's sleep. He had a busy day tomorrow, and he was tired of thinking.

After his shower, Gabe sat in his bed, restless, unable to sleep. His mind and heart thought of Dallas and nothing else. The draw to her pulled him from bed, but he couldn't step farther than the window. What had she done to him?

He was unable to see the house from his view, and it frustrated him. He wanted to see the house, her room, her smile, the light in her eyes as she teased him. He needed Dallas to love his daughter, to love him.

He looked at his clock on the nightstand. Thirty-eight more minutes before she left. He began to pace the bedroom. "Lord, what do I do here?" He continued to pace when he noticed a note on his dresser. As he neared, he realized it wasn't Cindi's handwriting scrolled across the paper with his name. That left one other person. He swiped the letter and unfolded it.

Gabe,

The last two years have been the hardest of my life, and honestly, I wasn't sure I was going to make it through if I didn't leave Graham. At the first opportunity that came along, I ran, and moved to Wyoming. But there was one snag, my house wouldn't sell no matter how many agents took over trying. It remained on the market without an interested buyer, until you came along.

Nine months.

I've thought about this before, but as I'm writing, I think I know the answer to why there wasn't anyone else interested in the house. I think the Lord was waiting for my heart to be ready to receive you and Cindi into my life.

His pulse roared within his veins, igniting his thoughts as to the possibilities of what she was saying. He read the last line again. Pacing, he continued to read.

If my words have thrown you like a bull, a little dazed and needing to catch your breath, it's the way I feel at times when we're together. It's the way I feel right now pouring out my heart. I'm not sure how you feel about us since we've never spoken about our feelings, but Cindi said something tonight that gave me hope. I admit, I hope you'll think of me. I will think of you and Cindi often. And I'd like to know you better when I'm away. I don't know what that will look like, but I'd like to try.

Sincerely yours,

Dallas

Not bothering with his shoes, he gripped her letter in his hand, grabbed his keys and cell, then headed out the door. Making sure the door locked behind him, he ran across the street and pounded on the door. He'd apologize later if he woke Ruth, but he needed Dallas.

The door opened and a tired Dallas stood there, eyes red, questions forming on her brow. "Gabe? Is Cindi all right?"

"Were you asleep?"

"No. I couldn't sleep."

"May I come in?"

"Yes. Yes, of course." He entered, and she closed the door. "What are you doing here?"

They'd barely reached the living room before Gabe took her hand within his, stopping them. He reached in his pocket and withdrew the letter, placing it in her palm. "I hadn't seen it until now. I have so many questions, Dallas. If I had time, I'd ask them, but you should know how I feel before you leave."

She looked at her hands, folding the letter at the creases. "I'm going to miss you. And it scares me."

"Then let me reassure you." He stroked a gentle finger along her jaw, lifting her gaze to his. "The Lord brought you into our lives. He knew how much we needed you, Dallas. How much I need you." He drew closer, allowing his fingers to have their way through her hair. Her eyes slowly closed, and he couldn't help but watch her lashes flutter with his touch. "I love you," he whispered, pressing a soft kiss to her temple, another falling to her cheekbone, then at the corner of her mouth. "I'll wait for you."

She turned those hazel eyes at him, so trusting, loving, it melted his heart. Her lips were hesitant against his, and he understood. If he had any sense, he'd be hesitant too, but this was it for him. There were no games, no misunderstanding, his heart and life were hers for the taking. "No pressure," he whispered near her ear. "I found you, Dallas. That's all that matters." She brushed her lips against his, and for a moment he held her there, taking the feel and breath of her in. He didn't answer her kiss as he wanted, but in a gentle response by tucking her within his arms. He wasn't sure how long they stood there holding on to each other, but when Dallas's phone rang, Gabe had a pretty good idea who was calling.

She moved from his arms, and he felt instantly cold. "Hello," she said. "Yes, let me grab my things. I'll be out in a minute." She ended the call and slid the phone in her back pocket and withdrew the letter she had written to him. She handed it back to him.

"Thank you." He took it and slid it in his pocket, then collected her suitcase from beside the newly placed loveseat and rolled it to the door. "Do you have everything?"

Her smaller luggage in her hands, she nodded. "Except for you and Cindi."

Her words surprised him. What he wouldn't give to get her to stay, but it had to be her decision. "We'll always be here for you, Dallas. Waiting for you to come home."

She took his hand, intertwining their fingers as they walked to the taxi. The trunk popped open as they neared, and Gabe slid the suitcases inside and closed the trunk.

She was waiting for him when he turned around, eyes large in the streetlight's beam. They were asking something of him. What? He didn't know, but whatever it was, he'd give it to her. Whatever she wanted to hear, he'd say it. "Dallas, you know I want you to stay, but if you don't, nothing changes for me—"

She leaned into him, pressing her hand against his chest, and with a gentle brush of her lips, kissed him. His lips responded, and the warmth from her palm branded his skin, straight to his heart. "You'll wait for me?" he heard her whisper.

"Never doubt." His voice was husky, but he didn't care. There was no shame in the way he felt, the desire to be married to this woman in his arms.

She smiled, running her fingers across his unshaved jaw. "I'll text you when I land."

"If you end up leaving. The longer we stand here, the more I'm willing to persuade you to stay."

Her smile widened as she slowly left his arms. "Then I better go so I can come back."

"To visit your aunt, of course."

"Of course."

He opened the car door for her and placed a final kiss on her cheek before she slid into the taxi. "I'll see you soon."

"We'll talk tonight."

He shut the door and waved as the taxi drove down the street and then turned out of view. Yet, he stood there, unable to move. "Lord, it's in your hands."

Landing at Jackson Hole Airport felt odd. Being back felt odd. Even now with her dear friend Penelope hurrying toward her. How was it that within days her future could have taken such a sharp turn in the opposite direction? It was as if she'd left herself behind in Graham. The only part she was sure she still carried with her was her caged heart. It pounded fiercely against its chamber and cried to return.

"Dallas!" Penelope hugged her. "It feels like you've been gone forever."

She chuckled. "Really? I can't believe I'm back so soon."

Her friend held her at arm's length and eyed her. "So soon? That's a new one."

"I know." She grabbed the handle of her luggage and led them toward the airport exit. "I'll tell you about my trip on the way to the ranch. I'm a little overwhelmed." How could she explain the warm look in Gabe's blue eyes when he looked at her, the same look that filled the broken and lonely places within? Or the way he loved his daughter as if she were a precious gift? Or how she was loved by both father and daughter and regretted leaving them? "Penelope."

"What is it, Dallas? You're worrying me."

She looked at her friend and then away. "I found something I never expected."

"What did you find?"

"Home."

EPILOGUE

*O*n videocall with Gabe, Dallas caught sight of her aunt and Cindi hurrying past the phone's screen. Once they were out of view, the call froze. "Gabe? Can you hear me?"

Holding her cell phone a little higher for a clearer connection, Dallas leaned back in her boss's office chair, missing the handsome man smiling at her from her cell phone. "Gabe?"

"Yeah, I'm here." The video unfroze, and he ran his fingers through his hair and patted it down on one side.

"Where are y'all going tonight?"

"There's a new restaurant someone told your aunt about that she wants to try."

How Dallas wished she was joining them, not stuck hundreds of miles away from the people she loved. "I miss you," she said, acutely aware how her heart had yearned for them since they'd visited during the rodeo that Jon had sponsored. She smiled at the memory. After the barrel race, Gabe and Cindi had brought her twelve red roses. He went on to tell her she'd been breathtaking out there, but the way his eyes had roamed her face and hair, she had felt his appreciation to the tips of her toes.

"You're smiling. What are you thinking about?"

Heat rose to her cheeks. "How after the barrel race, when you wiped the smudge of dirt from my cheek, you made me feel beautiful, delicate, and wanted."

"Which you are, and in five months, you'll be home for good."

A knock sounded, and she turned to find her friend peeking through the glass door.

"Hang on, Gabe." Dallas didn't want to let him go. "Penelope is knocking."

"Do you need to go?"

"Not yet. Just a sec." She turned back to Penelope and waved her in. Her friend's wide grin set her nerves on edge, especially with the change in her clothing. She wore a black knee-length dress, but before Dallas could ask why, Penelope took the phone from her and smiled at Gabe on the other end.

"How is it going, Gabe?" Penelope walked away from her and sat on the other side of the desk.

"Good. Aunt Ruth, Cindi, and I are about to head out for dinner. Dallas was tellin' me someone rented out the place tonight for an intimate dinner. She seems a little disappointed she's not singing or playin' the guitar tonight."

"Not disappointed, exactly." Dallas stood and went to Penelope. "Only when friends steal my phone." She shook her head and retrieved her phone. "I just enjoy what I do. Tonight, I'll be serving the party." She glanced at Penelope. "You both should see the white lights hanging from the ceiling and how the cabin is decorated. They took out the other bench tables and placed a large round one in the center of the room. Candles everywhere. It's going to be beautiful when it's finished."

"They're almost done decorating," Penelope said. "Jon sent me photos asking my opinion. It's going to be the highlight of some woman's night."

"Do you think it's an engagement?" Dallas asked, never having done an engagement party before, but the table seemed too large for an intimate moment for two people.

"Oh, I forgot the reason I came in. You need to get ready for tonight and dress up, Jon's orders."

"Me, in a sleigh, in a dress?"

"Yep. You got it." Penelope stole the phone once again. "It was great seeing ya. Tell that sweet girl of yours I said hello and we miss her around here. She lit up the place."

"Will do."

Penelope handed her back the phone. "Hurry," she mouthed, not too quietly.

"I suppose that's my cue." Gabe stood. "We'll be going too. Are we still on for date night tomorrow?"

"Absolutely. What do you want to do?"

"A movie? We can stream at the same time if the hotspot works."

"It's worth a try." She tightened her grip on the phone, her heart not into tonight no matter how much she tried. "I miss you."

"I miss you too. Not much longer until we're together again."

"I know." She took a heavy breath. "I'll call you tomorrow."

"Until then, goodnight."

"Night." She slowly ended the call. "I'll be in Graham in five months. To stay," she reminded herself. It had become her mantra when she thought about how the Lord had been working in her life.

She left the offices and headed for her cabin, aware the barns weren't clamoring with activity like normal. It was quieter with only one dinner venue operating to full capacity.

A sleigh passed, and she knew it was on its way to collect the guests for the party. She had to hurry and get out of her jeans, sweatshirt, and jacket.

Showered and makeup applied, she stood in front of her mirror and looked at herself in the dusty rose–colored dress. The color worked well with her light brown hair, and she loved the blend of vintage charm and femininity this full tea-length dress offered. She was glad she'd purchased it a few months back, because if she hadn't, she would have had to wear a more casual dress, and if what Penelope was wearing was any indication, she be underdressed. She grabbed her nicest coat and opened the door in time to catch Penelope and her fiancé, Dave, saunter toward her with wide grins. It had been hard for Dave when Ethan left for another ranch, but it had made way for him and Penelope to finally connect as they hadn't before. Their wedding was in two months' time, and Dallas couldn't be happier for them. "I'm ready! Thanks for letting me tag along."

"When has it ever stopped you?" Dave teased as he held out both elbows for them.

"Never," she laughed, taking his arm. With the heels she had on, and the cold at her ankles, she was grateful for the assistance. He led them to a two seated sleigh, drawn by two horses, she'd never seen before and which was parked out in front of Jon's office. "Where did this sleigh come from?"

"Oh, it's Jon's," Penelope answered as they neared the sleigh. She collected one of the red-and-black Sherpa blankets from the front bench and handed it to her. "He saves it for special occasions. The guests will ride back in it at the end of the evening."

Dave assisted her into the sleigh's back seat, then Penelope into the front. Her friend spun around to talk to her. "Remember, you're serving the guests. That's all. You'll arrive first and introduce yourself before the other guests arrive. Dave and I will hang back until the food is to be served."

Dallas nodded. "Sounds easy enough."

Dave grabbed her blanket, unfolded it, then proceeded to lay it across her lap, then Penelope's across hers. "My ladies." He gave an exaggerated bow. Dallas couldn't hold back her grin as he climbed into the sleigh beside Penelope. "Let our journey begin," he said, starting them off.

Penelope snuggled close to Dave and whispered against his ear. Dallas shut them out to give them privacy and took in the ride's view, wishing Gabe was here with her now to keep her warm.

It was a quiet drive through the lovely mountain valleys and one of her favorite times of the day. The only thing that could be heard were the horses' hooves crunching against the snow and the blades from the sleigh sliding against the patches of ice. In the last seven months since meeting Gabe and Cindi, this had been where she wrestled with her feelings of loving Gabe and Cindi and missing Keith and Lacy. The fear of moving on without them, and the fear of losing Gabe and Cindi as well. It was also a time when she wrestled with the Lord, giving Him the hurt and anger that she had held on to for so long. She needed healing, and she knew the Lord was the only One who could help her move on with her life.

The crisp air and the emotion in her chest caught her breath. All the fear and hurt that had been holding her back had been replaced over the months by the Lord's assurances that she'd found in scripture. He had a plan for her life, and though it might be difficult at times, He would never leave her. He also reminded her to trust Him and that He wanted to bless her. So now when she thought of Gabe and Cindi, she saw His hand from the first moment at the grocery store, to the coins in the attic, to her desire to be united to Gabe as his wife and as mother to Cindi.

But most of all, while she wrestled, her relationship with the Lord had been restored. He was the desire of her heart once again, and those broken pieces of her life and tattered soul had begun to heal. Her Creator knew the workings of her innermost being, and He was the One who tenderly wove His love between each piece, reminding her she was His, and giving her freedom to follow her heart.

And to make sure she was paying attention to what the Lord was doing in her life, her cousin Blade had offered for them to join forces to breed their stock and start their own horse ranch. She knew when she agreed what that meant: the Lord had secured her financial future, and how amazing it was that a childhood dream of hers and Blade's was finally coming to fruition.

She covered her mouth to stifle the laughter in her throat. *Thank you, Lord, for loving me.*

The four log cabins came into view, and Dave drove around to the right, where the smallest cabin rested in snow. A dull light shone from inside, but as they neared, she realized it must be the candles that were giving the cabin its soft glow.

Dave slowed the sleigh to a stop at the wooden ramp leading up to the front of the cabin. He stepped down and held out his hand for her. "Watch your step."

Dallas accepted with a slight bow of her head. "Thank

you, kind sir." She looked at Penelope, where she sat unusually quiet. Dallas was sure something—either joy or a joke—hid within her gaze. She wasn't sure which, but she didn't have time to find out with Dave's long strides ushering her from the sleigh toward the cabin.

He opened the cabin door for her, and, once inside, she began taking off her coat. Expecting Dave to give her further instructions, she turned to him, but he gave her a smile and closed the door behind him as he left. A little nervous at this new role of hostess, she hung her jacket by the door and ran her hands down her dress. Penelope said when the first guest arrived to just introduce herself, so until then she could just be in awe of the cabin's transformation. Dallas went around the cabin and admired the white lights hanging from the ceiling and the candles strategically placed to light up the darkest areas.

Her gaze caught on the lone table covered with a white cloth and the vase holding twelve roses that rested at its center. As she neared, she counted four place settings, each beautifully decorated, as if they belonged to a wedding reception.

Though everything was lovely, it was the roses that stole her attention. She couldn't help fingering one soft petal then another before she leaned over to inhale the sweet fragrance. She thought of Gabe and his gentle caress. "I'll be home in five months."

"To us."

Dallas spun at the sound of a man's voice, her palm against her chest. She froze, not sure if her mind was playing tricks on her, but her heart leaped at the sight of Gabe coming from the kitchen. "Gabe." He wore a tailored fit charcoal chino and a white button-down long-sleeve shirt under a black sportscoat. There was no tie, but the two top buttons were undone. His outfit matched the elegance of the room, and he looked good in it, but . . . "What are you doing here?" Her voice came out breathless.

"I missed you."

"You're supposed to be in Texas. I was talking with you a little over an hour ago. What about dinner at the place my aunt suggested?"

He shrugged, ambling over to her. "White walls and phone angles help to disguise where we were. And we've not eaten here before."

She regarded the table, and it took a moment to process what was happening. "This is for us? Cindi and Aunt Ruth are here?"

He studied her face, and his mouth quirked into a smile as he moved closer, running a hand along her arm. "No and yes."

She shook her head slightly. "I don't understand. Where are they?"

"We'll see them, but they're giving us time." He held her hand and ran his thumb over the inner part of her wrist, then lifted the tender skin to his lips. "This, my sweet Dallas, is for you and me." He pressed another kiss to her knuckles. "I've waited too long to do this." He drew her to the table with him and pulled a long stem rose from the arrangement, then went down on one knee. "For you."

Her breath caught as she accepted the rose. "Oh, Gabe."

"I want to make you feel like the woman you are, Dallas. Regardless if you're stompin' around in your boots, barrel racin', or exquisitely dressed like tonight, you are and will forever be beautiful and delicate in my eyes. You will always be wanted in our lives, hearts, and every day in my arms. I love you. I want to spend the rest of our lives together. Cindi and I, we need you."

Tears filled her eyes as he withdrew a mauve velvet box from the breast pocket of his jacket and opened the lid.

She pressed a hand to her chest at seeing the elegant rings. There were two, one a white gold band and the other a two-carat princess cut diamond. "Oh, they are so beautiful." She pulled her gaze away from the ring set to meet his. "But an engagement and wedding ring?"

"Dallas, will you do me the honor of being my wife, tonight?"

"Tonight?" she repeated, surprised. Penelope, that sly fox. She'd known. That's what Dallas had seen on her friend's face: joy.

"Yes, if you'll have me." Still on his knee, he looked up into her eyes. "I'm ready to start our lives together."

"But how? Do you plan on moving here for five months? Because I can't leave until then. I have a contract."

Gabe stood then and recaptured her hand. "We can stay for a week and have a honeymoon, but when I return to Texas, it will give us five months to find a home."

"Would you sell your home?"

"Our home. I can't sell it. It's part of who you are and your history. I'd rather rent it out and start our lives together in another home. Even build one if you'd like."

"You'd do that for me? You're being serious?"

He gave her a lopsided grin. "I've never been more serious in all my life. It's been seven months since we met, but when you called me a few weeks back and shared what the Lord had done in your heart and you couldn't wait to start our lives together, I got the ball rolling to be here. You'd mentioned a quiet wedding."

"I'm glad you brought Aunt Ruth and Cindi with you."

"Why wouldn't I? They'd like to see us married." He took her palm and pressed it against his heart. "So, what do you say? Will you marry me, tonight, and make me the happiest of men?"

She put her arms around his neck and kissed the corner of his mouth. "Are you sure you want to be hitched to me for the rest of your life?"

"Ball and chain, with no links in between. I love you being in my arms." He pointed to the other side of his mouth. "I think you missed a spot."

She laughed, leaning in to kiss the other corner. "Yes, I'll marry you. Tonight." At her words, his lips met hers in a sweet touch, and it filled her with such longing to stand next to him before the Lord to say their vows. "Who's officiating?" she asked, gazing deeply into his eyes, and witnessing the same love there as within her heart.

"Jon. Penelope said he was a pastor, and he agreed to marry us if you said yes. They're waiting for my text."

"Then maybe we should text them?"

Gabe grinned and held her close. With his other hand, he took out his phone from his pocket and began texting. "There," he said, tucking it away. "Penelope said Dave is bringing the sleigh around. Let me help you with your coat."

Dallas loved how attentive Gabe was being as he took her coat from the hook and held it open while she slipped inside. He hurried back to the table, where he'd set the ring box. The door opened, and Dave stood on the other side. His grin made her smile. He shook Gabe's hand and hugged her, wishing them both congratulations.

"Where are we going?" she asked.

"To one of the other cabins. Everything is ready, and Jon is waiting. Penelope can't believe you're getting married before her."

Gabe helped her into the sleigh, then sat at her side,

laying the blanket across their laps. Then they were off. "Dave, we could always have a double ceremony."

"And have her mother and father kill me?"

"Yeah, I see your point." Gabe turned to Dallas, and gently brushed his hand against her cheek, tucking several strands of hair behind her ear. "I love you, Dallas." His fingers lingered along her jaw.

She closed her eyes and savored his touch. "Thank you for waiting for me."

"How could I not when my heart already belonged to you?" The sleigh came to a slow halt, and Gabe helped her out.

As they entered the cabin, white lights and candles filled the space to match the other cabin. A seven-foot square arch adorned with Star of Bethlehem flowers stood at the far end, where Jon waited with a Bible in hand. Her heart soared at the reality that, within minutes, she was truly marrying the man she loved.

Wanting to hug Cindi and tell her she was thankful they were going to be family, she looked for her little girl and found her at Ruth's side. She caught sight of her aunt's wide grin and bright eyes, focused solely on her. She winked.

Yes, Aunt, you knew all along this was going to work out between Gabe and me, didn't you?

"Are you ready?" Gabe's smile grew, love shining in his eyes.

Oh, how this man stole her heart. "I'm more than ready."

~

FIVE MONTHS LATER

GABE DREW Dallas into his arms and kissed her hairline. "What do you think?"

She looked over the long wooden fence that ran along their new property and directly in front of their newly built home. Her pulse rose as she thought of her family—those at the Easton Ranch—and how they'd sold a large parcel of unused land to them to live on and to begin their own ranch. She and Blade had decided to keep five acres each to live on and use the rest for the horses. A month after she and Gabe married, the DGB Ranch came into existence. But it was Gabe who took the reins at building their house, with her giving input from Wyoming.

Now, standing on the property for the first time and gazing up at the ranch- style brick home, tears filled her eyes. "It's beautiful."

Gabe squeezed her hand. Oh, how she loved this man at her side. He'd not only worked tirelessly to make sure their house was ready before she arrived, but he'd opened his accounting business and started the wheels rolling to make DGB Ranch a dream come true. And he even took time to visit her in Wyoming whenever he could.

"Welcome home." Gabe's lazy grin warmed Dallas's heart as he turned her in his arms. "Mrs. Langston." He pressed his lips to hers in a gentle kiss, lingering. "I love you," he said against her mouth.

"I love you, Mr. Langston. More than I can express and—"

He bent down and lifted her off the ground, cradling her against his chest. Her arms circled his neck, and she giggled as he carried her. "What are you doing?"

"Takin' my wife over the threshold. We're doing this proper." He headed toward the house.

She chuckled. "You know you should have started to carry me when we were closer to the house."

"What are you trying to say?" He pressed his lips together in a mock frown, the sparkle in his eyes giving him away. "I'll have you know I've wrestled cows to the ground and rode some of the finest bulls on this side of the Mississippi River. I think I can carry a slip of a thing like yourself."

"My hero." She nuzzled his neck.

He chuckled and held her closer. "Hey, now, I said nothing about a distraction."

The front door opened, and Cindi stood there with a hand on her hip. "Finally. I want Dallas to see my room."

Gabe cleared his throat and gave his daughter a nod. "We'll be there in a minute." They glanced at each other and smiled. He strolled up the steps into the house, and he set her down in the foyer. He caught her hand and brought her knuckles to his lips before entwining their fingers and heading for Cindi's room.

Oh, how this man had stolen her heart when she wasn't looking. She couldn't believe how blessed she was and how gracious the Lord had been to them.

Now, she just needed to find a way to share they were expecting an addition to their family.

To discover more about the Eastons and the town of Graham, Texas, click HERE to travel back in time for adventure and the Wild West.

Sometimes the path to freedom is found in an unexpected future.

Upon the death of her mother, Rosalind Standford's life shatters, the pieces scattering to the wind when she is forced into a betrothal to a cunning banker. But when a telegram arrives announcing the man who captured her heart is on a train to Boston, Rosalind must hide her true feelings before the thin cord of her existence unravels the deadly secrets she keeps.

Cowboy Trent Easton returns to his roots in Boston society to find his childhood friend, the love of his heart. Instead, he finds a broken woman engaged to a man close to her father's age. Though she once rejected him, when Trent learns she's in danger, he determines to do whatever it takes to keep her safe—even taking her to the altar in the black of night. But will his name and the remote wilds of his Texas ranch be enough to protect her? Or will freedom cost them their lives?

EXCERPT FROM THE RESCUE

Charlestown, Boston
May 1886

*R*osalind Standford's heart thudded against her ribcage as she lifted her pale green ball gown and stepped into the foyer. *Where is he?* She stood on tiptoe and scanned the dinner guests, trying to catch a glimpse of Trenton Easton. Disappointment and the worry that had plagued her for the last few days clutched her. Was the gossip true?

Surely Trenton would have told her. Or her own mother, if she knew. Mother was the only person who encouraged Rosalind's feelings for her childhood best friend, feelings that had recently begun blooming toward something more.

Rosalind's stomach quivered at the thought. She ran her fingertips along silver threads and embroidered sequins at her waist. She'd picked this satin gown for Trenton, knowing it would accent her gray eyes, a trait he only last week said gave her a dove-like beauty.

Again she swept her gaze over the room, past her mother, her father—her gaze, unfortunately, snagging on that of Mr. Glover Richards, a man almost her father's age. He walked toward her, the click of his heels on the wooden floor lifting above the hum of scattered conversations and the hammering of her eardrums. She forced a smile and nodded, then turned to step away. His stiff, damp fingers slid around her upper arm, halting her movement.

A chill ran up her spine. "Mr. Richards." She pulled back.

His dark eyes narrowed, assessing. An amused smile twisted his lips. He bowed. "How are you this evening, Miss Standford?"

She trembled as her name slid past his thin lips with a hissing sound. It was silly, but she couldn't help herself. The man gave her the cold shivers. She didn't want to talk to him, let alone suffer his touch, though lately he'd spent so much time with their family he'd become hard to avoid. It was as if he and her father had become dearest friends. Manners demanded she give a polite response, but she couldn't bring herself to like the man. "Doing well, thank you. And you?"

"I'm grateful for your father's invitation to Mr. Easton's home."

"Being the bank's vice president has its advantages, does it not?" She folded her gloved hands and squeezed them together, wondering if Mother felt the same unease at Mr. Richards's constant presence.

"Indeed it does. It's my hope this new partnership between your father and me will secure more"—the corners of his mouth rose as if he enjoyed a private joke—"pleasant opportunities to come."

"I see," she answered, although she didn't understand his meaning. Father never spoke of business around her or her mother, but whatever the dealings, Mr. Richards seemed happy. "I hope you and my father have a great partnership."

Trenton descended the stairs, so handsome in his formal wear he took her breath away. He strolled past her, his jaw tense and his blond hair nearly touching his collar. Without looking to the right or left, he headed toward the dining room.

It's true. Trenton and his family were leaving Boston. The dinner was not a celebration but a final farewell. Tears stung her eyes. How could Trenton have kept this to himself? "If you will excuse me, Mr. Richards."

"Allow me?" He crooked his arm.

"Thank you, but no. My father is waiting." She hurried away before Mr. Richards could insist. Another minute with Mr. Richards might cause her to miss speaking to Trenton altogether.

She made her way across the crowded room, but the laughing, milling guests converging on the dining hall prevented her from reaching Trenton in time. Resigned, she joined her father and let him escort her into the dining hall. Music wafted in behind her while the spice of men's aftershave and the flowery scent of women's perfume clashed like cymbals. She reached the doorway and hesitated as dozens took their places in the wooden high-back chairs lining the tables. How many guests had been invited? She scanned the room. Fifty. Sixty. And they would all be finding out at the same time.

Her father escorted her to the table and selected for her the chair next to Mr. Richards. Mr. Richards stood, and his dark eyes met her father's with approval. Everything in her wanted to balk at not being seated next to Trenton, but her father's beaming smile gave her pause.

Throughout the meal, Rosalind pushed the roast lamb

around her plate, glancing at Trenton from the opposite side of the table, hoping her imagination had gotten the better of her. When Trenton's father stood at the head of the table and clanked his knife against his water glass, a knot grew within her throat.

"Ladies and gentlemen, I want to thank you for attending our gathering this evening. It is an honor to have our friends here on this night. As some of you have heard, there is gossip circulating that we are moving." Mr. Easton glanced at his wife and then his son. Trenton frowned. "It's true. The Eastons are moving to Graham, Texas. We leave tomorrow."

A collective gasp rose from the guests.

Rosalind bit her lip and forced herself to stay seated, though every part of her wanted to drag Trenton outside and confront him for not telling her. She deserved to know the truth.

Mr. Easton's parting speech seemed endless, and through its entirety, Trenton steadfastly avoided her gaze.

After supper, Rosalind headed to the balcony. It was warmer than usual for the time of year, and the other guests had gone to the ballroom, giving her a few moments alone to compose herself. Instead, she paced, thinking. Was there no idea she could offer? No sound reason to discourage the move?

She could find none, except those growing in her heart.

Blinking back tears, she stopped at the rail and looked into the night sky; the stars, like her mood, seemed dim. Even the rose-scented breeze—her favorite—failed to bring comfort.

"Why are you upset, little girl?"

Her heart ached. She'd know Trenton's voice anywhere. She turned toward him, her chin raised. "I am not little."

"Are you not shorter than I? And are you not a girl?" A smile played on his lips.

How she would miss his teasing. How she would miss *him*. "I am shorter, but I'm a woman. I'm sixteen. Women my age are married, I'll have you know. And if I wanted to be married, I would be."

"And who would you marry, Rosalind?" His voice lowered as he took a step closer. "Who would be able to keep up with a wife who climbs trees and steals chocolate bars?"

She planted her palms on her hips. "I didn't steal them. You laid them down in plain sight, and besides, you said I could have them."

"Only because you left me none."

Rosalind giggled, then it hit her again. He was leaving. Her hands slipped from her waist. "I'll miss you."

Trenton stared at his feet. She studied the top of his blond head until he lifted his blue eyes to hers. "May I write to you, Rosalind?"

"Yes. You better."

A heart-stopping smile lit his features, and a dimple appeared in his right cheek, stealing her breath. Whether what she felt was a mere crush or whether she was in love … well, with time, she'd learn her true feelings. Either way, she would treasure his letters.

She took a deep breath. "I guess I should go. Papa said we were leaving soon, but I wanted to come out here one last time." She slowly turned, forcing herself to go.

Trenton reached out and took her hand. "Rosalind, wait."

From the lightest of touches, her fingers warmed. Though propriety dictated she move away, she let her hand linger in his for a moment. Mother had told her a woman's feelings sometimes grew in baby steps, other times in leaps and bounds. What did it mean that she wanted to lace her fingers with his and never let go?

"What was the matter earlier?" He regarded her, squeezing her hand slightly. "You seemed upset."

"How long have you known you'd be moving?"

"I heard the gossip like everyone else, but I thought it was only gossip." His gaze moved to their hands. "Mother told me tonight, right before everyone came for supper."

"I feared you knew but didn't tell me."

He ran his thumb over her fingers. "I would have told you."

Heavy footsteps sounded behind them, and her hand slipped from his. "We're going, Rosalind," her father said. "Your mother is waiting for you by the door. She's feeling a bit ill."

"Yes, Papa," she called, then blinked back tears. "Until I see you again, Trenton."

"Goodbye, Rose."

Her heart squeezed as she walked away and followed her father out the door. Trenton had never called her "Rose" before, and she liked the sound of it. How long would it be before she heard it again? Would she ever?

She heard sputtering and gagging even before she saw her mother standing outside by another's carriage, one hand gripping Mr. Richards's arm, the other covering her mouth, her eyes wide and frantic. Father rushed to her side. Mr. Richards yelled for his driver to bring his own carriage around.

"Father, what is happening?"

Her mother coughed violently as the carriage wheels crunched to a stop before them. Mr. Richards assisted her father, but as they lifted Mother inside, her hand fell from her lips, revealing bloody fingers.

"Mother?" Rosalind trembled. *Dear God, please ... What does the blood mean?*

Mr. Richards came to her side and placed a gentle hand on her elbow. "Come, Rosalind. We must go."

She nodded quickly and allowed him to assist her inside the carriage. Her mother had been feeling poorly for months now and had tried to hide it, but the coughing fits had worsened. *God, take care of my mother.*

The hacking cough increased, and her mother jerked and writhed.

"Father, can we do nothing?" Rosalind asked. "Mother?" She looked from one to the other, but they both looked afraid and lost, an expression she'd never before seen on either of their faces.

When they arrived at the house, Father instructed Mr. Richards to find the doctor, and only after several stumbles did they manage to get Mother inside. Mother's strength had simply vanished, leaving her pale and aged, too weak to even keep her eyes open as they helped her to bed.

It seemed a lifetime passed before the doctor arrived. During the examination, Mother lay still. Too still. Fear surged to Rosalind's core at Mother's motionless state. Then another cough raked through Mother's body, blood dripped from her nose, and Rosalind didn't know which was worse— watching Mother lie still as death or seeing the spasms and hearing the awful retching. Tears filled Rosalind's eyes as she stroked strands of soft brown hair from her mother's face and tucked them behind her ear.

"Do you know what's wrong with her, Doctor? Is it consumption?" her father asked.

Kneeling next to the bed, the physician wiped her mother's nose and folded the cloth. "Her coughing is worse. I'm afraid you are correct. She has tuberculosis."

Rosalind shook her head and ran from the room. She flew down the stairs, faltered into the stagnant night air, and stopped on the porch as reality weighed heavily on her shoulders. She swallowed down her screams. "God, are You listening? Don't You see? You must help my mother. Please don't take her. Don't ..." She fell to her knees, sobbing into her palms.

Arms came around her shoulders, and she jerked back, biting back her tears. "Mr. Richards." She moved from him and stumbled on the hem of her gown but caught her balance.

"It's all right." He followed her. "I have your father's permission."

She wiped her cheek with the back of her hand. "What do you mean you have his permission?"

"We will be married."

Rosalind fought to understand what Mr. Richards was saying, but the words seemed scrambled, incomprehensible. Her mind a fog. "What do you mean, *married?*"

"Earlier tonight I asked permission to court you, but moments ago, he gave me his full blessing."

Surely she'd misheard him. "You asked for my hand in marriage now, while we're learning my mother is dying? My father is as distraught as I am."

"Perhaps the doctor's wrong," Mr. Richards whispered against her ear. "Perhaps she will recover. Nevertheless ..."

"We shouldn't be ... you shouldn't be alone with me here like this. Propriety ..."

He dragged a fingertip along her jaw, then down her bare arm, his expression declaring ownership even as it dared her to argue.

Though her heart galloped, she fought her instincts to flinch. Glover Richards was a very powerful man, she'd overheard her father saying once, powerful enough to harm his enemies. Father must need the man's friendship, otherwise he would never have agreed. "Why? Why me?"

"I will court you as your father wishes." A slow smile slid up one side of his face. "And at nineteen you will be my bride."

Rosalind's pulse pounded in her ears. None of this made sense. If only Mother were well. She'd never let Father agree to this marriage, and he would listen to her.

She balled her hands into fists at her waist, squeezing the satin lace crisscrossing there—satin meant to draw Trenton's eye. Yet Trenton was packing his trunk for Texas, even as Mr. Richards's gaze roamed her hair, her face and throat, and her bodice and cinched gown.

"We don't have to announce our betrothal ... yet," he said as if the deed was done.

She swallowed, meeting Mr. Richards's stare.

He took her hand and slid it through the crook of his arm. "Let's get you back inside, shall we?"

She let him lead her, but her heart recoiled, and she threw a desperate prayer toward heaven. *Lord, You must heal my mother and rescue me. Save us.*

For another story set in the town of Graham, Texas in the Wild West, click HERE.

When the sheriff's daughter goes into hiding from her father's killer, her life isn't the only thing in danger.

The day Jessica Thompson's father was murdered, she swore to never love another sheriff. Now, she's fleeing his killer. When her stagecoach is robbed and her rescuer declares she will be his wife, she does the only thing she knows to do—shove her revolver in his back. Never would she have expected he wore a star on his chest.

Sheriff Blake McKenny prides himself on protecting his town's people from danger, but his efforts don't include a headstrong woman bent on putting herself in harm's way. When outlaws threaten his town and put Jessica's life in danger, Blake's failure to save his late wife haunts him.

Can Jessica and Blake forgive themselves for the past and break down the protective walls around their hearts? Or will secrets and deception take their lives in a direction they never saw coming?

EXCERPT FROM THE PROPOSAL

Graham, Texas
1891

*B*lake McKenny's hand rested comfortably on the butt of his holstered gun as he leaned against an oak tree. Sweat trickled down his back—the shade did little good—but he loved it here. Several hundred feet away, the trees stopped, and wide-open prairie stretched straight to the sheriff's office in Graham, Texas, which lay a mile away, hidden by a gentle rise of land. God's country, he called it.

His office.

His land. Or soon would be.

He inhaled and silently said a prayer of thanksgiving. Seven years ago, he'd promised land to his wife—land he pictured them raising children on, land they'd work till they were old and gray. A promise he'd never been able to fulfill.

Not while she was alive.

He yanked off his Stetson and wiped his brow with his arm, thoughts shifting to the town meeting he'd left an hour ago in Fort Worth. Reports of stagecoach holdups—of men shot and killed while women and children were taken as captives to be sold to brothels—remained foremost in his mind.

He released a heavy breath. He had to find a way to keep the people in his town safe. But how could he stop outlaws, keep loved ones from dying at the hands of evil men, when he couldn't prevent his own wife's murder?

Images of long ago flashed in his mind for what seemed like the thousandth time. If only …

He shook his head against memories and pain as oppressive as the Texas summer heat and tried to refocus on his personal Garden of Eden.

In the distance, a stagecoach rounded a bend at a hazardous pace. He narrowed his eyes, tracking its movement. Two men rode up top—driver and shotgun. Dust billowed up from the ground around it, nearly obscuring the two riders galloping up from behind. The muscles in Blake's body tightened.

A light flashed in a rider's hand. The glint of sunlight off a pistol?

Four rapid booms answered his question. Was that a woman's scream?

Blake reached for his horse. He clenched the reins and leapt onto the saddle, scrambling for a plan.

The driver tumbled from the stage. The guard's body sank to the driver's bench, shotgun falling to the ground. The stage took a sharp turn.

Two bandits—one with a red bandana, one with a blue. He couldn't shoot them from this distance, having left his rifle at the office, but he could distract them. At this moment, any plan would be better than letting those in the stage be taken. Or worse, killed.

Blake rode toward the scene, pulling his bandana from his shirt pocket and quickly securing it over his face. Approaching the robbers from the opposite side of the runaway coach horses, he shouted, "Need some help, boys?"

He snatched the loose reins while Blue Bandana jumped from his horse onto the driver's box. Struggling to keep his balance, Blue Bandana yanked the reins from Blake and brought the team to a halt. The other rider, still on his horse, slowed beside his partner and pointed his gun at Blake's chest.

Lord, help me keep a cool head and save these people. Blake dismounted his horse and approached, hands raised once again, and eased toward them.

Blue Bandana on the stagecoach glared at him. The bandana had slipped to his neck, and Blake only caught a glance, one too brief to notice much.

Blake tipped his hat at the two. Their clothes were dirty and torn, but their guns—Smith & Wesson double-action—were clean. He'd seen revolvers like these only twice before. Thankfully, he was wearing one on his hip. "Heard the shots. Thought you might could use a hand."

Blue Bandana secured his disguise. "I'm afraid your rescue attempt was in vain, mister. We ain't tryin' to help nobody but ourselves."

"Stealin' is more like it." A hearty laugh came from Red. He kept his gun trained on Blake's chest.

Blake glanced at the stagecoach's door. If these men were the robbers who kidnapped women and children and sold them to brothels, he needed to do something and fast. He grunted and nodded at the stagecoach. "Take all you want. When I saw you both comin' in after the stage and heard a woman scream, I knew this was my opportunity. I'm here lookin' for a woman."

The man with the gun gawked. "Are you kiddin' me? Do you believe this, brother?"

Hard, dark eyes peered at him over the blue bandana. The robber had yet to jump down from the stage.

Blake strolled toward him as though he had all the time on this side of heaven. Hopefully, he did. "Let me take a look-see if there's a bride in here for me." He craned his neck to see inside the carriage.

One set of eyes—the color of a raging storm—glared back, brows knitted together above them. "Don't you dare touch me, or you'll regret it with your life."

Blake blinked twice. *Great.* He had a fighter on his hands. That's all he needed. "I'm in luck. I got me one *fine* filly in here." He turned back to the men.

A feminine but curt voice called out, "I'm not your woman."

"Brother, I thought you said there were no passengers?" Red, his horse antsy under him, shot a glance at Blue. "I thought one of the men sounded a little girly. There's a female in there."

The other threw the strongbox down with a thump. He jumped and landed a few feet from Blake. "Pull her out, stranger. I wanna see her."

Red chuckled, causing the gun still pointed at Blake's chest to shake. "If there's more, we could have a little fun."

Blake's jaw ticked. They knew this stage was carrying a strongbox, but not about the woman? Maybe they weren't the bandits he was looking for. Losing the strongbox with its wages would be difficult, but to a much lesser degree than losing this woman. Blake had a chance to save this from going bad. "She's the only one." Praying this woman wouldn't get him shot, Blake swung the door wide and waited, but backed against the opposite side of the carriage, she made no move to emerge.

Not having time to explain his actions, Blake reached in, grabbed her wrist, and pulled her out the door, helping her as much as possible but being rougher than he would have liked. He'd apologize later, but now he needed to play the part. Their lives depended on it.

She tumbled forward, and though he tried to catch her fall, she landed hard on the ground. He was tempted to apologize and collect the travel hat and satchel by her side, but needing to keep up the pretense, he yanked her to her feet. Her brown hair unwound from its bun and fell like silk across her smooth face. Not helpful for her cause. Neither was the becoming flush on her cheeks.

He snatched her hat off the ground and crammed it on her head in a sad attempt to hide her pretty face. "You know what's expected as a bride," he said. "Do as you're told."

Sparks of lightning seemed to shoot from her eyes straight at him. He opened his mouth to speak, and she spat in his face.

Red pointed his gun and snickered. "Well, I'll be. Look who we have here."

Blake shifted to face both men and kept the girl behind him, slipping the gun from his holster. Blue Bandana stepped toward him. "She's mine," Blake growled. "If you plan to die today, then take another step."

Something solid jammed between Blake's shoulder blades. "Are you hard of hearing?" The woman behind him spoke in a tone that shook with anger. "I am not now, nor will I ever be, yours. Toss aside your weapon."

Heat flowed through his veins. Here he was, trying to save this woman, and look where it got him. A gun in the back. "Easy with that thing, ma'am."

"I'll be easy when your gun is on the ground! Everyone's guns on the ground." The subsequent clicking sound spoke of how serious she was.

"Sure, sure." He released the cock on his own weapon and dropped it at his feet.

"Well, what a nice turn of events." Red Bandana chuckled. "C'mon, brother, we got what we came for. More money than we've ever seen in our lives. She ain't worth it."

Blue set his sights on the woman yet again. His gaze intensified, almost as if he knew her. Blake was tempted to turn around to study her for himself, but he held his stance.

But then the robber stepped back and cut the lines that hitched the horses to the stage. With two guns pointed at him—one from the woman, the other from Red—Blake stood and sweated a river while Blue Bandana heaved the strongbox onto one of the freed horses and secured it in place.

Finally, the bandit swung into the saddle of his own horse. With a wink for the woman, he shot a round into the air. The remaining stage horses jolted into a full gallop, taking Blake's horse along with them. The bandits followed.

Blake ground his teeth. If only he could use his gun on those murdering thieves, but no—he had a gun to his back. It took all the patience he could muster to wait for the men to leave, especially Blue, who turned his horse back for another look before disappearing over the horizon.

Blake had to get his horse back, but first he'd have to deal with the metal digging into his flesh. "Your turn. Put down your gun."

She hooted. "Not on your life."

Time for a new strategy. "I must warn you, if you shoot me, you'll be hung for killing a sheriff."

She laughed again, distrust tainting her voice, giving him

the impression she wasn't going to lower her gun. Blake hated to manhandle her more, but he had no choice. He wasn't ready to die today. Shifting his body weight to one side, he caught a glimpse of her arm. He'd wait for the right moment.

"Where's your badge, lawman?"

Of course, when he needed his badge, he didn't have it. If his deputy could see him now, Blake would never be able to live it down. "It's in my desk drawer. At the sheriff's office."

"Your first mistake, mister. A sheriff never forgets his badge. I've seen men like y—"

Blake twisted, grabbed her wrist, pulled her forward, and yanked the gun from her as she flew past him. She spun mid-flight and fell to the ground on her backside. After opening the revolver, he dumped the bullets into his palm. "I'm sorry to do that again, but ..." He looked down.

Those dark eyes sent daggers his way for a second time, but this time, he was sure one stabbed him in the heart. Never had he seen a woman with such fire, such ... beauty.

She jumped up, balled her fists, and held them up as if she planned to fight him.

He couldn't help laughing. No. Never had he seen a woman like her. "Ma'am, you have two choices. Ride back to town with me or walk, but I have a feeling I know which choice you'll take. However, if those men return, you won't be so lucky." Blake pocketed the bullets and slid her revolver into the belt of his pants. Turning, he scanned the stage, and at seeing the lifeless guard, yanked a blanket from under the bench and covered the body.

The woman looked away, swallowing hard. "Ride?" She searched the ground. "On what horse?"

Blake realized what she was looking for and snatched her satchel from the dirt, then handed it to her. He drew his lips together, letting loose a shrill whistle to call Legend to return if he was still within earshot. "I need to look for the driver. You stay here." He holstered his discarded pistol and walked toward the area where the driver had fallen.

"What's your name?" A softer, gentler voice sounded from behind him.

He didn't turn around. "Blake."

"Is that it? Just Blake?"

He couldn't understand this woman. One minute she was trying to kill him, and the next she acted like she cared. "Why do you want to know? To write it on my headstone?"

From the south, Legend trotted to him and stood like a soldier, waiting for his command. Blake ran his hand down the horse's mane, collected the reins, and then continued his search for the driver.

"No," she said. "When I get to Graham, I'm going to find out who you really are."

"Blake McKenny." He spotted a crumpled body ahead near the trail. Dropping the reins, he ran to the man and felt for a pulse. Weak. But at least there was one. Blake wrapped his bandana around the man's bleeding head, then looked over his shoulder to find the woman holding his horse's reins. "He's alive but needs a doctor. I've got to get both of you to town." He rose and strode toward the horse.

She climbed into Legend's saddle, moving the horse farther from him. "I'll head into town and let the doctor know where to find you. It'll be quicker." She guided the horse into a canter, leaving him standing there.

Blake exhaled. Surely this woman would drive any man insane. Especially him. He had to get help, but there was no way he'd leave her alone given what had happened here or what he'd learned in Fort Worth. Her riding off unaccompanied into dangerous country wasn't an option either.

He allowed the woman her lead as he dragged the driver to partial shade under a mesquite tree. That done, he drew his lips together and whistled. His horse circled and trotted straight for him. He didn't mask his smirk as she approached. Or when one of her hands fisted as his horse stopped directly in front of him. Or when he took the reins and climbed up behind her.

It was the moment he realized how perfectly she fit against his chest that his smirk fell.

MORE ABOUT TANYA EAVENSON

Tanya Eavenson is an award-winning Christian romance novelist. She enjoys spending time with her husband and their three children. Her favorite pastimes are grabbing a cup of coffee, eating chocolate, and reading a good book. You can find her at her website, Facebook, or at her readers group, Tanya's Books & More.

ALSO BY TANYA EAVENSON

GAINING LOVE NOVELLA BOOK TWO

Pediatrician Patrick Reynolds works wonders with sick children, yet when it comes to pets, he's clueless. But caring for his sister's menagerie while she's on vacation is the perfect answer to working through a broken engagement. Hoping to escape the memories, he returns to his hometown, the last place he'd expect to find love. Life as a single mom is never easy, but pet shop owner Amabelle Durand has found contentment. When an old friend returns to care for his sister's pets, he enlists her assistance to keep the animals alive. But when Amabelle's young daughter falls ill, she finds herself attracted to more than the handsome pediatrician's medical skills. As Valentine's Day approaches, will Patrick and Amabelle miss out on the love they've always desired? Or will their love take flight under the stars on this very special night?

GAINING LOVE NOVELLA BOOK THREE

Undercover agent Madi Reynolds has spent years infiltrating a human-trafficking ring, but when her life is threatened, she is advised to leave the country with her bodyguard. War Veteran and ICE agent Brice Johnson has been defending his country and American lives for as long as he can remember. Now, he faces the biggest assignment of his life—protect the woman he loves. He's never been one to run from a fight, but when crippling visions of war call out to him, he begins to wonder if surrender is an option after all.

To Gain Forever

GAINING LOVE NOVELLA BOOK FOUR

Karianne Bennett, small-town wedding coordinator, has always believed in happily-ever-afters. That is, for everyone but herself. But then hope comes when she adopts a retired service dog and a cat-walking newcomer catches her eye. Trey Scott has been fascinated with fireworks since he was a boy. If he can land the festival account in an out-of-state town, he'll be that much closer to achieving his lifelong goal. His dreams never included a beautiful dog walker who also happens to be the stranger he's been praying over for years.

GAINING LOVE NOVELLA

Undercover ICE agent, Brice Johnson, fell in love with his partner, but the fight to control his PTSD drove him to leave her and his assignment. Deep undercover, ICE agent Madi Reynolds' identity is blown, and she is involved in a hit-and-run meant to kill. Lucky to be alive after her vehicle was forced off the mountain, she finds herself in a wheelchair and facing an unknown future. Unable to forgive himself for Madi's accident, Brice vows to protect her, but is it enough?

The Heart of Mercy

GEORGIA PEACHES NOVELLA BOOK FOUR

Mercy Cunningham runs a homeless shelter and soup kitchen in Atlanta. Dismissive of her noble work among the destitute, her father continually pesters her to work for his Fortune-500 corporation. A bedraggled stranger visits the soup kitchen and catches Mercy's attention. Not because of the piercing gaze almost hidden behind his facial hair, but because something seems off about him.

Noah Allen is not the pastor, or even the man, he once was. The single-blow death of his wife and child made sure of that, as did a raging opioid addiction. Blaming himself for their deaths, he wanders the country without a destination and without a desire to find one.

Then, Mercy finds him.

UNENDING LOVE SERIES BOOK ONE

Elizabeth Roberts can't remember her past, and the present is too painful. She turns to nightclubs and drinking to forget her infant daughter's death, her husband's affair. When his wife's coma wiped out the memory of their marriage, Chris Roberts found comfort elsewhere. He can't erase his betrayal, but with God's help he's determined to fight for Elizabeth at any cost. She wants to forget. He wants to save his marriage. Can they trust God with their future and find a love that's unconditional?

Restored

UNENDING LOVE SERIES BOOK TWO

Dr. Steven Moore is known nationally for saving lives. If only he could save his own. Unable to deal with his prognosis, he retreats to a happier time in his past—to the woman who once stole his heart. Four years after the death of her beloved husband, bookstore owner Elizabeth Roberts still struggles to sustain her faith and joy in the Lord as she raises her two sons. She strives to find a way through her family's grief, never suspecting a man from her past might offer hope for her future. But how can there be a future when he's only come to kiss her and says good-bye?